"Isn't this great, Daddy?"

"Yes," he said, "it is." And he made a mental note not to get too used to it. Isabella had brought Savannah home and then stayed to help watch her so he could work, something that probably most of his friends in Claremont would've done. He didn't need to think anything more of it than that, and he shouldn't feel guilty about enjoying this time with her so soon after Nan's death. She was a friend, helping them out by cooking a meal. That was it.

Isabella motioned toward the three place settings. "I kind of invited myself to have dinner with y'all," she said. "Is that okay?"

He pushed Savannah's chair in so she could reach the table better and then took a step toward Isabella. Titus assumed his emotions had been obvious, if she'd have even considered that he might not want her to stay. After everything she'd done for him, everything she'd done for Savannah, he wouldn't ask her to leave.

Plus, he wasn't ready for her to go.

Renee Andrews spends a lot of time in the gym. No, she isn't working out. Her husband, a former All-American gymnast, co-owns ACE Cheer Company. Renee is a kidney donor and actively supports organ donation. When she isn't writing, she enjoys traveling with her husband and bragging about their sons, daughter-in-law and grandsons. For more info on her books or on living donors, visit her website at reneeandrews.com.

Books by Renee Andrews

Love Inspired

Willow's Haven

Family Wanted

Her Valentine Family
Healing Autumn's Heart
Picture Perfect Family
Love Reunited
Heart of a Rancher
Bride Wanted
Yuletide Twins
Mommy Wanted
Small-Town Billionaire
Daddy Wanted

Visit the Author Profile page at Harlequin.com for more titles.

Family Wanted

Renee Andrews

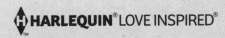

HARLEQUIN® LOVE INSPIRED®

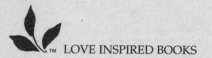

LOVE INSPIRED BOOKS

ISBN-13: 978-0-373-81854-9

Family Wanted

Copyright © 2015 by Renee Andrews

www.Harlequin.com

Printed in U.S.A.

The Lord is my light and my salvation.
Whom shall I fear? The Lord is the stronghold
of my life; of whom shall I be afraid?
—*Psalms* 27:1

For Brother Wayne Dunaway, my preacher and the inspiration for Brother Henry in all of the Claremont books. I appreciate your love for the Lord and your willingness to share your vast knowledge, particularly with young and upcoming preachers. We have been blessed that our sons have had the privilege of studying with you.

Chapter One

Dear Titus, hurting you was the last thing I ever intended to do.

Isabella Gray drove beneath the wooded canopy leading to the future home of Willow's Haven, trepidation shimmying down her spine. An orphanage. The man she'd promised to see *had* to be building an orphanage. Oh, they might call it something different, a "child home," but Isabella wasn't fooled by the tender name.

She pushed aside memories of the past—dark rooms and muffled cries, a hungry stomach and filthy sheets—and focused on what she planned to do. She'd talk to Titus Jameson. Once that was done, she'd never set foot near another orphanage—or child home—

again. Then she'd leave Claremont, Alabama, and go...

Isabella had no idea where to go. Certainly not back to Atlanta. But after she talked to this man, she'd start her new life. New location. She'd dreamed about living in a small town, a place where everyone knew everyone's name and cared about each other. She'd read about those tiny towns, but Richard hadn't thought them worthy of a visit. Throughout their ten years of marriage, Isabella asked repeatedly if they could take a trip to one, but Richard never understood her desire or the point. What would his colleagues think if he vacationed in some Podunk hole-in-the-wall town? He had an image to maintain, and he wouldn't taint it trying to satisfy her whimsical idealization of small-town America.

But now that he had a new wife to help him preserve his image, Isabella could finally do those things she dreamed of. She'd get a job. She had a degree, after all. Surely she could find some form of employment, even if she'd never worked a day in her life.

The thickness of the woods shrouding the long, gravel driveway gave the impression that the trees were closing in, and the unwanted yet familiar trickle of claustrophobia seeped through Isabella's veins.

The Lord is my light and my salvation. Whom shall I fear? The Lord is the stronghold of my life; of whom shall I be afraid?

She breathed in, absorbed each word of the verse that had seen her through the scariest years of her childhood and continued down the darkened driveway. Ten minutes ago, she'd admired the brilliant sunshine of the June afternoon, the expanses of cotton, soy and corn fields bordering the road leading to Claremont like a patchwork quilt welcoming her in her quest to do the right thing. But now, as the trees closed in, she didn't feel welcomed. She felt warned. And she considered turning the car around and leaving without sharing information with a man she'd never met.

But she didn't want to break her promise to the woman who had provided Isabella with the dearest friendship she'd ever known.

She'd expected to find a construction crew working on-site, but there was no sign of anyone except a guy riding a bulldozer on the opposite side of the property. A trailer sat on its own to the right. She assumed that was the makeshift office. She parked beside a navy pickup with a Jameson Construction Company magnet stuck to the driver's door.

Time to see Nan's ex-husband. Her heart thudding loudly in her chest, Isabella climbed out and made her way toward the trailer, but a man in a baseball uniform opened the door before she had a chance to knock.

"Oh, hello, I'm Brodie Evans." He waved her inside. "You must be here about the ad in the paper. Savvy said she got a couple of calls from people wanting to interview. Come on in. I'm heading out, but she's on her way down from our place. She'll talk to you about the job." He motioned to the tiny living area. "Have a seat."

Isabella sat on the sofa, not so much because she wanted to but because she needed to gather her thoughts and figure out what was going on. However, before she could ask questions, the door burst open and a teenage boy entered. "Hey, Dad, we're gonna be late if we don't leave now."

"I know." Brodie pointed to the teen. "This is our son, Dylan."

"Hi," Dylan said.

"Dylan, this is…" Brodie let the word hang. "I'm sorry. I didn't get your name."

"Isabella. Isabella Gray."

"Nice to meet you," Dylan said, holding out his hand.

Bewildered, she didn't know what else to do but shake his hand. "You, too."

Then the door opened again, and two little girls entered, their bright-eyed faces and blond pigtails so similar that Isabella wouldn't have been able to tell them apart.

"Hey, Daddy," they chimed, energy bristling as they bustled in. "Hey, Dylan." Then they noticed her and one asked, "What's your name?"

"I'm Isabella," she said, as a blond woman and another little girl entered.

The third little girl was about the same size as the other two, probably the same age, but she had long dark hair and a solemn disposition, as if she'd gotten in trouble before they arrived.

"Isabella, this is my wife, Savvy," Brodie said. "Savvy, this is Isabella Gray. She's here about the job."

"Hi. Let me get the girls situated and then

you and I can chat." She turned to Brodie. "Y'all need to get going, don't you?"

He kissed her cheek. "Heading on out," he said. Then to Isabella, "Nice to meet you."

"Nice to meet you, too." Isabella knew she'd need to set the record straight soon, but from what she could tell, Titus Jameson wasn't in the trailer. Maybe he'd already left for the day and the company truck she'd seen had been driven by the guy on the bulldozer.

"One second." Savvy held up a finger to Isabella and then turned to the girls. "Rose, Daisy, y'all take Savannah to the playroom and show her your new dolls."

"Come on, Savannah." One of the girls grabbed the quiet one's hand and tugged her to the playroom.

Isabella didn't get a good look at the third girl's face, because she never took her attention from the floor as she walked, the same way Isabella had walked around the orphanage when she was about the same age. Sad. Lost.

What had happened to that little girl?

She couldn't hold back her curiosity. "Is she okay? Savannah?"

"I can tell you're going to be good at iden-

tifying the children who need special attention," Savvy said, her voice barely above a
whisper so the girls wouldn't hear in the next
room. "That'll be important if you work here,
even if you're in the office. We want everyone to care about the children and understand
that they'll need plenty of love to make it
through the hard times." She glanced toward
the playroom and sighed. "Savannah is visiting our girls today. Her mom left her and
her dad a few years ago, and even though I
wasn't living here and didn't know Savannah then, her father said she's never been the
same. She does seem to enjoy playing with
Rose and Daisy, though, so I plan to keep
inviting her over and offering to watch her
whenever I can."

Isabella nodded, glad that the little girl still
had her father and that she also had friends in
Rose and Daisy, and a tenderhearted lady like
Savvy watching out for her. Isabella hadn't
had anyone watching after her back then.

She started to tell Savvy that she hadn't
come for the job, but before she could speak,
a knock sounded and then the door opened.
Isabella's breath caught in her throat as a construction worker entered wearing an olive-

green T-shirt with Jameson Construction on the left of his chest, well-worn jeans and boots. She'd seen construction workers before, but none had ever looked like this. In fact, she would say he was way beyond nice looking. He was riveting, in a rough-and-rugged, outdoorsy and all-out-masculine kind of way. His hair was dark, a little longer than she'd have thought she would like, but she did like it, very much. And he had the kind of fit physique that you'd expect to see climbing the side of a mountain in a Mountain Hardwear ad. Was *this* the man from the bulldozer?

Isabella didn't know what was happening to her senses. She wasn't the type of female to ogle a good-looking man. In fact, one of Richard's complaints had been that she was too reserved, a little distant even, when she first saw or met strangers. And it wasn't as if she was looking for a man to fill some void in her life. She *didn't* want another relationship. At merely eighteen, she'd allowed her attraction for Richard and everything he offered to lure her into a marriage that never should've happened.

So she resolved that she'd get a firm grip on this sudden yet undeniable fascination.

* * *

Titus had been clearing land at the site for Willow's Haven since sunup, yet he'd only finished the space intended for the first cabin. At this rate, it'd take him until the middle of July before he had the place ready to break ground. But he wouldn't complain. He'd prayed for work, and God had granted his request in abundance.

This year, he'd take Savannah shopping for new school clothes come August, a luxury he hadn't been able to afford last year due to the economy's plummet and the limited span of construction needed in Claremont.

Entering the trailer, he glanced around and saw no sign of his little girl. Savvy, however, stood a few feet from the door.

"Hey, Titus."

"Hey, Savvy. I'm done for today. Savannah been okay?" What he wanted to ask was if she seemed happy, if she smiled, or if she at least joined in to play with the girls.

"Of course. She's precious."

Not as much information as he wanted. This morning's call from the latest child psychologist had informed him that the woman didn't know what else to do for Savannah and that she believed Savannah would work her own way out of the depression. But, like all the others, she hadn't told Titus anything about when or how that'd happen.

"I appreciate you watching her today, but we should probably be getting home now."

Savvy's eyes held a hint of sympathy, the same type of look he'd received often since Nan left. "Rose and Daisy enjoy playing with her. You bring her anytime. In fact, they'd love it if she came every day this summer while you're working here. It helps me out when they have company because it keeps them entertained."

He wondered how much entertainment Savannah could provide if she was as solemn as she was at home, but it would help him to bring her on-site, so he said, "Thanks, I will. And let Brodie know I finished clearing the site for the first cabin." He paused for a moment, suddenly aware that they weren't the only ones in the room. He'd been so interested in learning about Savannah's day that he hadn't noticed the woman sitting on the sofa in the living area. But now he couldn't take his eyes away. She had long, auburn hair that fell in subtle curls past her shoulders.

Though she was seated, Titus could tell she had petite features and wasn't very tall, and she had eyes as vividly green as the forest in the spring.

Titus was around pretty women often in Claremont. Typically, he barely noticed more than their names. All of the women from town knew him as Savannah's father and, more importantly, Nan's husband. And as the man whose wife walked out on him three years ago. This lady didn't know him, so she obviously didn't see him that way, and yet there was something in her manner of looking at him—almost as if she could see directly to his soul and that she "got" what he'd been through. "Hello," he said.

She shifted on the sofa, as though his greeting made her a little uncomfortable, which only intrigued him more. Then she moistened her lips and said, "Hi."

"Oh," Savvy said, showing her palms as she began her apology, "I'm so sorry. I forgot a proper introduction. Isabella, this is Titus Jameson. He owns Jameson Construction in Claremont, and he's the best builder around. Titus, this is Isabella Gray."

"Nice to meet you," he said, with an inexplicable desire to know more about the stranger. "And if you want the truth, I'm the only builder around." He'd hoped to elicit some response, but she merely stared at him, green eyes studying him with such inquisitiveness that Titus wondered how much she already knew. But Savvy had introduced him as though she hadn't mentioned Titus.

Then why did he see so much compassion and a hint of confusion in the stunning lady's eyes?

"Daddy?" Savannah entered the room carrying a piece of construction paper. "I made this for you." She held it toward him, a crayon drawing centering the page.

"Hey, sweetie." He took the paper, and his mouth tensed before he managed a slight smile. "That's a good picture." He pointed to the tall stick figure on the page. "Is that me?"

She nodded.

"And that's you?" he asked, indicating the smaller figure with dark hair down her back.

Another nod.

"And that says…" He hesitated, pointing to the letters across the top—*MY FAMLE*.

"My family," Savannah said softly.

He tenderly brought his arm around her,

pulled her close and kissed her cheek. "That's a nice picture," he said, his heart breaking at the lonely image on the page.

She didn't smile but moved her head against his shoulder in agreement.

Titus suspected Savvy knew how the drawing affected him and—he glanced at Isabella again and saw that she looked as sad as he felt—it seemed Isabella also understood. How, he didn't know, but the concern was evident on her face.

Titus wanted to talk to her, to find out why she seemed to care so much and also to determine why, when they'd barely met, he was drawn to her more than any woman in the past three years.

It'd been a long time, but Titus knew this feeling, remembered it well. Had missed it but also felt guilty having it.

Attraction.

Isabella watched the touching interaction between father and daughter and finally got the chance to see Savannah's face, the younger face of her dear friend, and she knew she couldn't go through with her promise.

How could she tell this man everything

Nan had said about him and then also tell him that she'd never muttered a single word about their little girl? A little girl who reminded Isabella so much of herself at that age. Lost. Confused. Abandoned by someone who should've stayed, who should've loved forever.

Isabella barely contained her tears as she watched Titus and Savannah leave. But she held it together. She had to. Because while she may have come here to tell Titus what Nan had said, she had a different reason for being here now.

That little girl needed help. And Isabella knew how she felt, probably more than anyone else.

After they left the trailer, she said to Savvy, "I'm interested in the position." *And*, she silently added, *I want to help the little girl Nan left behind.*

After telling Savvy she wanted to apply for the job yesterday afternoon, Isabella had promised to bring her résumé by today and then she'd driven through Claremont, as tiny as Brodie Evans had depicted. A town square centered everything and seemed to be the place to go last night, with lots of people shopping and visiting, children playing around the fountain, elderly couples chatting on wrought iron benches.

She'd needed something to cheer her up after leaving Willow's Haven. Although she'd decided God had sent her here to help with the child home and Savannah, she'd still been so brokenhearted and confused.

Nan hadn't told her everything, and Isabella couldn't figure out why. How had her friend left that precious little girl behind? Or that man, a hard worker and such a sweet daddy? And, have mercy, undeniably breathtaking, too. Nan certainly never told her that. Isabella hadn't been able to get the images of him off her mind.

Titus, all muscled and impressive, reminding her how it felt to experience instant attraction for a man. Titus, dropping to one knee to talk to his sensitive little girl. And Titus, looking at Isabella as though he could see into her heart, as though he might actually understand the pain of her past.

She thought of his daughter, Nan's daughter. Savannah had looked as forlorn as Isabella had been at that age. Nan had known how much that hurt Isabella, not having a mom around. Isabella had told her. She'd confessed *everything* about her childhood. She'd thought Nan was the first true friend she'd ever had and that they'd shared everything.

Isabella had. Why hadn't Nan? If Isabella had known that Savannah was here, she'd have made Nan get in touch with Titus so Savannah could have seen her mom one more time.

Last night, she had seen so many children with their parents on the square. True depictions of family. And she'd thought of Savannah's drawing, the two figures so alone in the center of a plain white page.

"Nan, what were you thinking?" she asked, driving toward the child home.

She'd prayed for guidance before she started this journey, and when she'd ended up at the charming Claremont Bed-and-Breakfast on Main Street last night, she hadn't questioned that God directed her path. She'd take the job at the child home, assuming Savvy offered it, and if everything went as well as she expected, she'd move her things from Atlanta in a month or so. She didn't want to be too hasty in her decision to relocate, but in her heart she already knew that this was where she should be.

Within fifteen minutes, she knocked on the door of the trailer with her résumé in hand. She'd awakened before dawn and spent over an hour searching the internet for résumé guidelines and then generating her first one. And she felt very good about the business administration degree listed under the Education heading. Richard had enrolled her in the University of Georgia as soon as they'd returned from their honeymoon, saying that his colleagues wouldn't understand if his wife didn't have a proper education.

She'd been so eager to please him that she hadn't objected, because she assumed she'd be able to use the degree to obtain a job. However, Richard only wanted her to be educated—he didn't want her to use the education. A wife who worked meant her husband wasn't successful enough to support them on his own. And he wouldn't have any part of that.

Isabella knocked again, but no one answered. Then she heard a vehicle coming up the driveway and turned to see Titus Jameson arriving in the same navy pickup she'd seen yesterday. She held up her hand in a wave, and he did the same, parking the truck next to her car. Nan had been a stunning lady; Isabella should've known she'd have been married to an equally gorgeous man.

But...*wow.*

He climbed out and opened the door of his extended cab so Savannah could exit.

Isabella watched them, her heart skittering in her chest at the sight of him in the green work shirt, blue jeans and boots. He'd looked good yesterday when he was soaked with sweat, but he looked incredible all cleaned up and ready for a new day, too.

"Nobody there?" he asked, as he and Savannah neared.

"I guess not," Isabella said.

"Probably running some errands."

Isabella nodded. "I can wait." Then she looked at Savannah, clutching a doll in one hand and a small pink bag in the other. Isabella placed the résumé on a deck table by the door and put her purse on top of it to keep it in place. Then she sat on the top step to talk to the little girl. "What do you have there?"

She looked at her daddy, and he touched her back. "Go ahead and tell her what you've got."

Isabella patted the spot beside her and was pleased when Savannah sat down. "This is Bessie. She's gonna play with Rose and Daisy's dolls."

"That sounds like fun," Isabella said. "I like her brown hair. It's like yours, isn't it?"

Savannah frowned. "I want mine like Rose and Daisy's," she said, "but I can't do it, and Daddy can't, either."

Isabella then noticed that the underside of Savannah's hair looked matted. She apparently had made the effort to create a ponytail, and it had ended badly. "Would you like for me to try to do it?"

Savannah looked from Isabella to her daddy. "Daddy said Miss Savvy could," she said. "Do you know how?"

"I think so."

Savannah handed over the pink bag, her small fingers gently brushing Isabella's palm with the action. "This is what Daddy bought for my hair. It's got a brush in it." She unzipped the bag and withdrew a pink plastic brush. "You unfold it like this and then you brush with it." She popped the pink brush out and locked it into place, then handed it to Isabella.

"Okay. Why don't you sit here in front of me, and I'll see what I can do."

Savannah's mouth lifted in a subtle smile, and she glanced at her father before turning and sitting on the step in front of Isabella. "Sometimes it hurts when Daddy does it, and I cry."

He frowned and shrugged. "That's true."

Isabella was touched by the relationship before her, a daddy so concerned for his little girl. What would it have been like to have had a parent care that much?

"Well, let's see if I can manage not to make you cry today." She thought about the statement and then added, "Not that your daddy did anything wrong, but I've had a little more practice." She glanced in the pink bag and saw a teeny hairbrush at the bottom. "Look, there's a little brush for your doll." She fished it out and then handed it to Savannah. "Why don't you brush her hair while I brush yours?"

Isabella was obviously a natural with children, and it touched Titus immensely that his little girl already seemed to be warming to her.

Savannah rubbed her hand down her doll's

hair as Isabella gently drew the brush through the top layer of Savannah's long brown hair. Then she lifted that layer and flinched at the mess. Apparently, Titus flinched in reflex, and Savannah noticed.

"Did I make it too bad?" She twisted around to look pleadingly at Isabella. "Can you not do it now?"

"No, I can do it," Isabella said. "I'll just take my time." Then she tenderly worked her fingers into the knot to loosen it before she tackled it with the brush. "Do you go to school yet?" she asked, obviously still trying to get Savannah's attention on something besides her tangled hair.

"Not now. Now it's summer," Savannah said softly.

Titus watched as Isabella eased her fingers through, the knot appearing to give a little with her effort. "That's right. How could I forget that? But before it was summer, did you go to school?"

Savannah nodded, which must have caused her hair to pull, because tiny tears crested the bottom of her eyes and trickled free. "Ow."

Titus flinched again. He couldn't help it.

Isabella couldn't see Savannah's face,

but she saw his and leaned forward to spot Savannah's tears. "Oh, dear, I'm so sorry about that."

"That's okay." Savannah blinked a couple of times and tried to act older than her age, the way she'd often done since that day when she'd been forced to grow up overnight, the day her mother left.

Titus watched her visibly compose herself to speak, another quality she'd learned since their world fell apart. "I was in kindergarten last year," she said. "This time I'll be in first grade."

He was pleased that she wanted to communicate with Isabella. Typically, she remained silent unless absolutely necessary, so seeing her engage in conversation was a huge step. He thought about calling the child psychologist and relaying the event, but he'd already decided they weren't going back. Besides, that woman hadn't been able to get Savannah to utter more than a couple of sentences during the entire time they'd been going to her. Isabella had her talking in a mere day. Obviously, this woman was special, and Titus said a prayer of thanks to God for sending her their way.

"What was your teacher's name?" Isabella asked, while Titus continued enjoying the vision of his little girl slowly but surely creeping out of her shell.

"My teacher was Mrs. Carter," Savannah said, "but I don't know who my teacher next year will be yet."

The knot released, and Isabella grinned as her fingers moved all the way through. "I think I've got it," she said, then took the brush again and gently pulled it through the mass of hair. "You've got a lot of hair, don't you?"

Savannah turned toward Isabella, her eyes wide. "Mommy said that, too."

Titus fought the emotion pulled from her words. He could almost see Nan, sitting on the couch with Savannah seated in front of her on the floor. They'd often watched television together that way, with Nan brushing Savannah's hair.

"Well, your mommy was right," Isabella said. "So, do you want a ponytail, or do you want two pigtails, like Rose and Daisy had yesterday?"

"Two pigtails."

"All right then." Isabella parted the hair down the middle, then gathered it into a pigtail on each side while Titus watched, amazed. She made it look so easy, but he had no doubt that if he tried, he'd probably have a worse tangle than the one Savannah had created this morning. Unlike Rose and Daisy's pigtails, which were short and curly, Savannah's were long, draping well past her shoulders.

But he knew the length of her pigtails wouldn't matter to Savannah. What mattered was that she had something like her friends, and Isabella had helped that happen.

"All done," she said, looping the elastic band around the second pigtail.

Savannah pulled a small mirror with a princess on the back from her bag and held it out to see each of the pigtails. She turned and gave Isabella the smile that Titus had been waiting for. "Thank you."

"You're welcome," Isabella said, and then, while Titus's heart squeezed tightly in his chest, Savannah scooted closer and put her arms around her in a hug.

"I'm gonna play with Rose and Daisy today," she said, her voice more cheerful than Titus had heard in a very long time. Then she glanced toward Titus and added somberly,

"I'm supposed to go to swim lessons tonight, but I don't think I want to."

His jaw tensed with his disappointment. "You don't want to give it another try? That was only your first lesson last week, sweetie. You might like it better this time."

"I want to swim," she whispered, turning her attention from him to the doll in her hands, "but I'm afraid."

Titus's gaze caught Isabella's, and she looked as though she understood that he had no idea what to do, what to say, to help his daughter.

Then her eyes brightened, and she gave him a smile before telling Savannah, "You know what? I taught swimming lessons when I lived in Atlanta. Maybe I could help you learn to swim."

Savannah's eyes lifted. "But I'm scared. I really want to, though."

"We would go very slow," Isabella said, "and I'll be right there with you, if you decide to let me help." She paused and then added, "I sure would like to."

"What do you think, Savannah?" Titus asked. He said to Isabella, "I'd be happy to pay you for private lessons, if that's what you're offering."

She shook her head. "You wouldn't need to pay me. I'm happy to do it. And I didn't get paid for teaching in Atlanta. I volunteered." She shrugged. "It's something I enjoy."

"What do you say, Savannah?" he asked, throwing in another quick prayer for God to set this in motion.

She took another look in the mirror at her pigtails, then turned to Isabella. "I'll try."

Isabella wrapped an arm around her and gently squeezed. "That's great." She looked to Titus. "You'll have to let me know where the nearest pool is."

"John and Dana Cutter just put in a pool at their dude ranch, and they told me I could bring Savannah to swim anytime. I'm sure they'd be fine with you teaching her there." He couldn't believe this change of events, this incredible breakthrough with his little girl.

"That sounds great," Isabella said. "Just let me know when y'all are ready to start."

"You think I can learn it, Daddy?" Savannah asked, and he hated that he still heard hints of doubt and fear in her voice. "That I can swim?"

He gave her a reassuring smile. "I sure do," he said as Savvy's truck appeared in the driveway. She, Rose and Daisy waved as they parked beside Isabella's car.

Seeing Savannah, the girls wasted no time climbing out. "Hey, Savannah! I like your hair!" one said.

"Me, too," the other said. "And I like your doll. Do you want to bring her inside to play in the toy room? Our dolls are already there."

Savannah looked at Titus, and he nodded his approval. "Go ahead," he said. "Have fun." Savannah gave Isabella a little nod before following them inside.

"I appreciate you offering to teach her to swim," Titus said after the girls entered the trailer. He appreciated it more than she'd ever know. Her kindness had placed a crack in the tough shield Savannah had set in place after Nan left.

"I'm looking forward to it," she said.

"You teach swim lessons?" Savvy asked.

"I volunteered teaching swim lessons in Atlanta and loved it." She pointed to the paper beneath her purse. "I included it on my résumé, even though it isn't office experience."

"It's experience helping children, so it's

totally applicable for this job. And who knows? Maybe we'll build a pool here for the kids eventually. If you're gonna dream, might as well dream big, right?"

Titus looked toward the trailer. "Right," he said, and he realized that his dreams for Savannah may have started coming true today.

Thank You, God.

Chapter Two

Sometimes, God gives us tough decisions to make, and maybe I made the wrong one.

The main room of the trailer had a small kitchen to the left, a couple of desks in the center forming a workspace and a tiny sitting area to the right with a sofa and television. "You brought your résumé?" Savvy asked, guiding Isabella to the kitchen table.

"I did." Isabella handed her the piece of paper.

Savvy scanned it as she spoke. "After you left yesterday, I realized I never told you the history behind Willow's Haven. Brodie reminded me that it's important everyone who works here knows how the place has come about and the reason behind our desire to help children."

Isabella had wondered what caused Savvy and her husband to start the home. "Were you orphaned?"

"Technically, no," Savvy said, "but my mother abandoned me when I was born and left me to be raised by my grandparents. I was fortunate, because my grandparents are amazing, but there are a lot of kids who are abandoned by their parents and have nowhere to go, which is why we'll help children who are either orphaned *or* abandoned. That's the reason we're classified as a children's home, rather than an orphanage."

Isabella could hear the compassion in Savvy's voice as she talked about the home, and it touched her heart. "It sounds amazing," she said, praying she'd get this job and have an opportunity to be a part of something that would truly change children's lives. "Where did you get the name, Willow's Haven?"

"It's named after my best friend, Willow Jackson. This trailer was her home." She took another look at the résumé and glanced up at Isabella. "Willow passed away a little over a year ago and left her children to me.

Brodie and I couldn't get over how much love Dylan, Rose and Daisy needed after Willow died, and we couldn't stop thinking about the children who didn't have anyone to provide that love. We knew there were orphaned and abandoned children who didn't have anyone who would talk to them about things that are truly important, like faith and God."

Isabella's throat tightened. She'd never had anyone mention faith *or* God in the orphanages she'd lived in. She'd latched on to every snippet of God's love that she'd learned on the rare occasions she'd gotten to attend church, primarily at Easter and Christmas, and that was only because those were the times the churches gave cash to the orphanages or foster homes. But those tiny glimpses of God, whenever she got them, saw her through the hard times. Gave her hope. Even if she'd seen Richard as something of a savior when she'd been eighteen.

"So the plan for Willow's Haven is to provide a Christian environment where children will know that they are loved by the staff and, more importantly, by God. And our ultimate goal, of course, is to place each child in a loving, Christian home."

"That sounds incredible." Isabella wondered how different her life would've been if she'd have been placed somewhere like Willow's Haven. Would she have responded so quickly to all of the attention Richard Gray provided?

Savvy's dark eyes practically sparkled with excitement. "I know. We were so blessed that Ryan Brooks and Dana Brooks Cutter—the brother and sister at the head of Brooks International—thought so, too. Their company is funding the child home. And I was so excited to hear from you so soon. I just placed the ad three days ago."

Isabella didn't want to lie about seeing an ad that she still hadn't laid eyes on. "I believe God led me here."

Savvy's mouth lifted on one side. "I'm thinking you may be right." She pointed toward the kitchen. "I made a pot of coffee earlier. Would you like some?"

"Sure, but I can fix it." Isabella served herself a cup of coffee with plenty of cream and sugar. "You want some, too?"

"Already had three cups." Savvy held up the résumé. "You have a business administration degree, but it doesn't appear that you've used it."

"No, but I'd like to."

Savvy looked as though she wanted to ask more about the degree but then thankfully moved down the page. "Okay, I see your volunteer work teaching swimming at the Y, but this says you've also been volunteering at the charity hospital in Atlanta, up until last week?"

Isabella sipped her coffee, enjoyed the delicious warm liquid on her tongue. "I put the name of the administrator under my references. I really enjoyed working there, volunteering there, I guess I should say."

Savvy wrote something on the paper. "What made you start volunteering at those places, and why did you leave?"

She'd started volunteering at the Y because Nan told her she'd enjoy working there. Nan had held a paid position as an office assistant at the Y until she was too sick and went to the hospital, where she met Isabella.

Isabella wouldn't tell Savvy about her relationship with Titus's ex-wife, so she focused on the other reason she'd started volunteering. "My husband—ex-husband—and I divorced last year. I wasn't feeling very good about myself at the time, and I wanted to do something to help others while I waited for the divorce to be final. Then I planned to move away, find a small town and start my life new, away from the big-city lifestyle."

"You don't get much farther away from big-city than Claremont," Savvy said, grinning.

"I realized that last night, when I went to the town square." Isabella recalled the quaint Mayberry-type atmosphere that radiated from the place.

"And so your divorce just finalized, and you were looking for a small town where you could settle down?"

"No. It was final six months ago, but I…" She struggled to say enough, without saying too much. "I became friends with one of the patients at the hospital, and I didn't want to leave until—" she carefully picked her words "—until she no longer needed me."

Savvy's hand moved to her heart. "You're going to be great here, you know. You may even be perfect to oversee a cabin eventually, but having you in the office will work, as well."

Isabella wanted her to understand how

much she already felt drawn to Willow's Haven. "I was raised in orphanages," she said. "And they were terrible. I won't go into detail, because I honestly don't want to think about it—or talk about it—ever again. But when you described what your plans were for Willow's Haven, I felt like God brought me here for a reason. Because I *know* how children feel when they're abandoned, and I know how important it would've been to me to have someone who cared, someone who told me about God and someone who truly loved me."

Two thick tears trickled down Savvy's cheeks, and she brushed them away. "I knew God answered my prayers with you," she said softly. "I'd like to go ahead and show you everything today, what computer software we've bought for the office, the files that we're going through in our search for children needing a home. There are plenty of kids— too many, truth be told—but we want to be ready to take as many as we can as soon as possible. As the cabins go up, we want to fill them." She motioned toward one of the small desks with a laptop. "Everything's over there. We'll go ahead and get started. Sound good?"

"That sounds great." Eagerness flooded Isabella's soul. God had brought her here. She could feel it. And she couldn't wait to get started.

"I thought it would," Savvy said. "And while you're figuring things out, I'll call your references. But I already know that everything will be fine."

Happy with this turn of events, Isabella took her coffee and started across the room as the phone on the desk began to ring. "Do you want me to get that?"

"Sure," Savvy said. "Just answer, 'Willow's Haven.'"

Isabella picked up the phone on the third ring. "Willow's Haven," she said. "Can I help you?"

"Well, ma'am, I hope you can. I'm trying to get in touch with a Mr. Titus Jameson. I called his office, and the voice mail left this number. Would he happen to be there? It's rather important."

"Yes, he is. Hold on one moment, and I'll see if he's available." She lowered the receiver and said to Savvy, "It's a gentleman looking for Titus. He said it's important."

She nodded. "His cell doesn't pick up out here. Let me see if I can get him."

Isabella waited while Savvy went outside. She heard her calling Titus's name, and then she returned.

"He wasn't far away," she said. "He's coming."

A few minutes later, Titus entered, his forehead already starting to dampen with sweat and his work shirt beginning to cling to his muscled frame.

Isabella handed him the phone while trying not to stare.

Not an easy feat.

"Thanks," he said, his fingertips brushing hers in the exchange.

"You're welcome." She didn't want to blush, but she thought it might be happening anyway, so she turned her attention to the laptop in front of her, even though the only thing on it was a screensaver of Dylan, Rose and Daisy.

"This is Titus," he said.

Isabella heard the other man's voice, a distant mumbling through the receiver as he spoke to Titus, but she couldn't make out the words. And she really didn't want to eavesdrop on the conversation, so she moved the mouse around on the computer with the hopes that something would show up besides the screensaver.

Savvy had gone to the kitchen area and started washing dishes. But since Titus took the call at the desk, and there wasn't a whole lot of room for him to walk around and talk with the cordless, he simply sat in the chair opposite Isabella and listened to the man on the other end.

Which made it easy for her to see when the color drained from his face.

"She's...dead?" His eyes slid closed and he remained silent for a moment, while the other man's muffled words continued to sound through the phone. Then Titus took a deep breath and answered, "No, I'm not her brother," he said, his words slow and deliberate, as though he struggled to get them out. "I'm her husband."

Chapter Three

I thought I could handle anything, that we could handle anything, but I learned my limitations.

It'd taken Titus six days to gather the right words to tell Savannah that her mommy would never come back. The phone call from the hospital had sucker punched him, and he hadn't known how to deal with the blow. Nan had been sick. Dying. And he hadn't even known.

And his "closure" had been pathetic. Pitiful, even. Nan hadn't had a funeral. An online memorial page had been set up by the hospital for guests to sign. There weren't even any pictures. According to the guy from the hospital and the memorial page, Nan had chosen to donate her body to science in the hopes of curing the rare kidney disease that killed her. That, of course, was the type of thing the woman he knew and loved would've done.

But what had happened to Nan between the time she left and the time she died? He'd learned from the memorial page that she'd worked at the Atlanta inner-city YMCA before she'd gotten sick, but that was all. She'd had an entire new life that he knew nothing about.

During the past three years, he'd been confused. Hurt. But for the past six days, he'd been angry. And oddly enough, his anger hadn't been focused on Nan but on God. How could He deal Titus this blow? How could He have turned his back so thoroughly on Titus and, even more, on Savannah?

Savannah. He hadn't been able to stop thinking about his little girl. She was already so sad from Nan's abandonment, but now he couldn't even offer her hope of seeing her mommy. And he wondered if he'd ever see her happy again.

But each time he doubted whether she could recover from all this, he thought of the way she lit up each morning when Isabella talked to her about what she planned to do to her hair. And he thought about the way she played with Rose and Daisy and the fact that those two little girls had lost their own mom not that long ago.

He knew Savannah *could* be okay, but it wouldn't happen on its own, so he had to get out of his own funk and help his little girl. He'd hesitated about asking Isabella to do more than fix her hair each morning, because he couldn't stop the feeling of guilt he experienced each time he was around her. He'd been attracted to her, *very* attracted to her, even before he learned of Nan's passing.

Truthfully, he still was.

But his little girl had connected with Isabella, and he had the perfect means to allow them to intensify that bond and to help Savannah cope with this new pain of Nan's death. Savannah wanted to swim, and Isabella had offered to teach her. Titus hadn't done anything about that because he'd felt wrong for being attracted to Isabella at all. But he had to put his daughter's needs first, so he'd deal with this attraction…and ask Isabella for help.

"My mommy is in heaven now."

Isabella glanced up from the laptop to

see Savannah, clutching the same doll she'd brought to the trailer each day since they'd first done hair together last week. She looked hopefully at Isabella as though expecting some kind of perfect response to the statement. Not knowing where this conversation would go, Isabella said a quick prayer for guidance and then said, "Yes, she is."

A couple of blinks, a chew on her lower lip, and then Savannah added, "Daddy is sad."

Isabella knew that was an understatement, since Titus hadn't said a word about his wife's passing since the phone call last week. In fact, each morning he entered the trailer, hugged and kissed Savannah before she started playing with Rose and Daisy and then worked like a madman until the sun went down. "I know he's sad."

And undoubtedly shocked, too. Isabella had also been shocked. That phone call had overturned the main thing she'd thought she knew about Nan. Titus hadn't been her *ex-husband*; they were still married when she died. Isabella had no idea why her friend had lied about something like that, and now that Nan was gone, she'd never know.

She wanted to help Titus cope with the loss,

but she barely knew him and certainly didn't know what to say about his wife's death. It wasn't as if she could now tell him that she'd known Nan and had been with her, holding her hand, when she died.

The trailer door opened, and the twins bustled inside, their chatter quickly filling the room. "We got the stuff to make grilled cheeses," Rose said, as Savvy followed them in with a bag of groceries she'd retrieved from their cabin. Rose and Daisy had asked to tag along when she went for the items, but Savannah had said she wanted to stay with Miss Isabella. She'd done this often over the past few days, asking to stay at the trailer with Isabella instead of leaving with the girls.

"My mommy went to heaven," Savannah said to Savvy, in much the same sorrowful tone that she'd made the statement earlier.

Savvy glanced at Isabella before she responded, her features softening and her eyes glistening with unshed tears. "I know, sweetheart. And I'm sure she's happy there." She forced a smile. "Everyone is happy in heaven."

Savannah nodded and chewed her lip again while Rose and Daisy, completely oblivious to the conversation occurring in the kitchen, discussed which dolls they would play with first.

Isabella prayed Savannah would eventually be that happy again. And she also prayed that she could somehow make that happen. She also wanted to help Titus, but he clearly didn't want to be helped.

Then again, he was still in the mourning stage, in spite of the fact that he hadn't seen Nan in three years. Titus apparently dealt with his grief by working. And not speaking any more than necessary. He also hadn't come to church Sunday, which had surprised Brodie and Savvy. They said he and Savannah were there every time the doors were open, so when Isabella agreed to visit the Claremont Community Church with her new friends, she'd expected to see him. That didn't happen, which also made her question if he might be blaming God.

So much to wonder about the intriguing man, but not a whole lot to know for sure, since he was bound and determined to remain in his shell.

God, be with Titus. He's hurting. We all can see it, and I'd really like to know what to do about it. He's been dealt some terrible blows, and he's such a hard worker and good daddy to Savannah. Please heal his heart, Lord. And if it be Your will, let me help.

She frowned, wondering if she should've prayed for God to let *her* help. Helping might mean getting closer to the man, and she'd been burned too badly by Richard to want to get close to any man again, even a man as intriguing as Titus. So she amended her prayer. *God, let someone help him. And if it be Your will, let me help Savannah.*

There. That prayer felt better.

"Why don't y'all go play with your dolls while I make the sandwiches?" Savvy said to the trio of six-year-olds, pulling Isabella away from thoughts and prayers about Titus. "I'll call you when they're done."

"Okay, Mommy. Come on, Savannah," Daisy urged, taking Savannah's arm and tugging her toward the playroom.

Savannah followed, her feet dragging in her traditional manner of reluctantly joining in the fun.

"Go on," Isabella urged. "You'll have a good time."

Her shoulders lifted a little, and she followed the other girls into the playroom.

"I'm worried about her." Savvy unwrapped the orange cheese slices and placed them on a plate near the stove.

Isabella moved to the refrigerator to retrieve the butter, then took her spot beside Savvy to spread it on the bread. The two of them had quickly grown accustomed to working together each day, whether on the computer going through the files of children needing a home or taking care of the twins and Savannah. She enjoyed having someone to talk to, to feel normal with. It reminded her of the way she'd been able to so easily talk to Nan.

And it reminded her that she shouldn't tell too much. She'd shared everything with Nan, but Nan had kept many things—important things—from Isabella. Things that were causing her problems now, because she felt extremely guilty withholding the truth from Titus. Especially since Nan asked her to tell him how she felt.

But instead of sharing all of that with Savvy, Isabella simply said, "I'm worried about her, too." She paused and then added, "And about Titus."

Savvy placed the buttered bread in the skillet, the scent filling the tiny kitchen as the sizzle penetrated the air. "The way I see it, he lost Nan twice. The first time when she left them with no more than a note, and the next time when she died."

Isabella had learned tidbits about Nan's departure over the past week, mainly from little things Savvy said, but she'd had no idea her friend had left her husband with a note. "A note? She just left a note and then walked out?"

Savvy placed a square of cheese on each slice of bread and then Isabella topped them with another piece of bread. "I probably shouldn't have said that, since I didn't hear it from him, but it's fairly common knowledge around town. So sad."

And so unlike the Nan that Isabella had known, so caring and kind. So still in love with her ex-husband. Correction...husband.

The trailer door opened, and she turned to see the object of her thoughts stepping inside. Savvy also turned and quickly asked, "Titus, do you want some lunch? We're making grilled cheese sandwiches, and I can easily make a couple more."

"No thanks," he said, his brow furrowed and his jaw tense, as though he were debating what to say.

"Is everything okay?" Savvy asked. "Did you need to talk to Brodie about the land? He and Dylan went to the college for the baseball team's practice, but I might be able to get him on the phone if you have a question."

"No, I don't have any questions," he said. "Everything is going fine with the clearing. I should make it to the third cabin's site by tomorrow."

Isabella noticed that, though he answered Savvy's question, he never took his eyes off of Isabella. Her skin prickled under his gaze. During the handful of times he'd come to the trailer each day, Isabella fought the impulse to stare. He was such a mesmerizing man, with his long dark hair, the tan skin of a guy who worked outdoors, hazel eyes that only seemed to emphasize the depth of the pain he felt at his wife's abandonment and then her death.

Isabella was drawn to him in spite of their limited conversations, and she found herself staring again. But this time, his attention seemed as focused on her as hers was on him.

"I do have a question, though, for Isabella," he said, then looked toward the hallway that led to the playroom. "I'm also going to take the rest of the day off and spend some time with Savannah, if that's okay."

"That's fine. You've been working much longer days than Brodie and I ever intended," she said, grabbing a spatula and flipping the sandwiches.

Isabella's pulse had skittered when he said he had a question for her. The fact that he still hadn't asked it made her wonder if he'd learned the truth. Did he know that she'd befriended Nan? And that she hadn't been honest with any of them about her reason for showing up in Claremont? Was he going to ask her to stay away from him? Stay away from Savannah? Because she couldn't think of a thing that would hurt her heart more.

"You want to ask me something?" she finally managed.

"Can we talk outside?" His voice seemed even deeper, full of emotion, and her skin prickled again.

God, please, let him forgive me.

Isabella followed him outside, her shoulders dropping and feet dragging in much the same manner as Savannah's.

Fighting his attraction to Isabella was going to prove more difficult than he thought. Even now, with the way her green eyes studied him as he led her to the small table on the deck, Titus found himself wondering what those eyes looked like when she was blissfully happy. Maybe even what they looked like when she was in love.

He swallowed past that thought. He had no business thinking anything of the sort, and he'd get a grip on it right now. He'd just lost his wife, and he needed to concentrate on helping his daughter.

She took a seat across from him at the table but had barely sat down before she asked, "Are you okay? Did I—do something wrong?"

He should've realized she might think that, should've thought about her feelings, but it'd been three long years since he'd been around a woman enough to truly remember how sensitive their feelings are. Something else God had allowed: Titus had grown numb to observations of the opposite sex that should come naturally.

"I'm sorry," he said, at least remembering that apologizing was always a good start to rectifying acting like a typical male. "You didn't do anything wrong. In fact, you've been the most right thing about the past week. Savannah looks forward to getting here each day so she can spend time with you."

"I'm glad for that." Her soft smile, which did reach her eyes and happened to show him how pretty she was when she smiled, lifted his spirits and gave him the push to go forward with this conversation.

"That's what I wanted to talk to you about," he said. "Before I learned what had happened to Nan, you mentioned teaching her to swim. She hasn't said anything else about it, but I think that's because I've been…well…I haven't been as approachable for her over the past few days. I'm sure she can sense that I'm dealing with a lot, because she finally asked me if *she'd* made me sad last night, and so I had to tell her the truth." The memory of her question, delivered quietly before bed, stabbed his heart. His brooding had caused her to feel she'd done something wrong.

"She told us that her mommy went to heaven," Isabella said, her voice barely above a whisper, as though she knew how sensitive this topic was for Titus.

He appreciated her even more for that. "Is that all she said?" he asked, wanting to know everything going on in his little girl's mind after learning her mommy had died.

Isabella's hands were folded, resting on the wooden table, and she looked at them instead of Titus. "She also said that you're sad."

He closed his eyes and considered praying but canned that idea. Chances were, he'd end up telling God how he really felt about all of this, and there wouldn't be anything good to come from that. "Six years old and she's lost her mom, yet she's worried about me."

Isabella looked at him again, her mouth lifting a little. "That's what girls do."

Another reminder that he'd become clueless when it came to females. For his daughter's sake, he'd do his best to remember. "About the swimming…"

"I still want to teach her," she said, and she sounded almost excited about the idea, which touched an even deeper spot in Titus's heart.

She really wanted to help Savannah. "When do you want to start?"

He wouldn't wait any longer. "How about today?"

Chapter Four

I've met someone...

"Can I just go see Abi and her horse again?"
Savannah's eyes, as wide with fear as a
spooked stallion, locked onto Isabella's, probably to keep from looking at the water. It was
the same look she'd given her the past three
days each time Isabella entered the pool...and
Savannah remained firmly on the concrete.

Though Isabella had worked with children
who were afraid of the water in Atlanta, she'd
never encountered a child as terrified as Savannah. And she'd never seen a parent so tormented by his daughter's fear. Titus looked
to Isabella and nodded, letting her know he
agreed that they didn't need to push his little

girl. "Sure," Isabella said. "But I'll stay here by the pool, in case you change your mind."

Savannah shot a wary glance toward the blue water and then turned toward Titus. "I'll swim tomorrow," she said quietly, identical to the way she'd made the statement the past three days.

He forced a smile. "Are you sure you want to try again tomorrow? We don't have to come back if you don't want to."

And, like the other times, she nodded. "Yes, please."

"All right then." He handed her the pink T-shirt and shorts she'd worn over her swimsuit. She put them on and slipped her feet into her shoes before heading toward the pen near the barn where Abi Cutter currently rode her pony, Brownie.

Isabella knew there was no need to remain in the water. Savannah wouldn't try again today. She fought the impulse to feel as discouraged as Titus looked, watching his daughter literally run away from her fear. "Maybe tomorrow will be better," she said, as she started out of the pool.

He'd been sitting beneath a purple umbrella at a circular wrought iron table near the shallow end, where Isabella had attempted to coax Savannah in. He stood, picked up Isabella's colorful striped beach towel from the table and held it toward her as she reached the edge. For the past two days, he'd sat nearby, smiling when appropriate, offering his frightened little girl encouraging words but obviously torn apart over her fear.

"Should I keep this up, Isabella? She says she wants to swim, but should I keep bringing her here? Putting her through this? And putting you through this, too?"

She accepted the towel and wrapped it around her as she prayed for God to give her the right words. She had so much admiration for Titus Jameson, and something else, too. A longing to comfort him, to see him happy again. Even now, standing so near to him, close enough that his woodsy scent tickled her senses, she wanted to offer him more than words. She wanted to hold him, tell him that she was sorry for what Nan had done and let him know that he didn't have to go through this alone.

"You aren't putting me through anything," she said. "I'm here because I want to be here, and I do think Savannah will work her way through this eventually."

Titus cleared his throat. "I read online last night that children aren't inherently afraid of the water. It's their life experiences and the attitudes of those around them that generate that fear. Savannah used to play in the kiddie pool at home all the time until she was three, so I'm afraid that Nan's leaving has something to do with this fear. But she wants to conquer it, and I want to help."

"I want to help her, too," Isabella said. He had no idea how much. In fact, she wanted to be the kind of person to Savannah that she'd always wanted for herself growing up. Someone she could depend on. Someone she could trust.

"I can tell that you do, and I appreciate that more than you could know." His shoulders lifted as he inhaled, and then he pointed toward the round table. "Do you have time to stay for a few minutes and talk while she's visiting with Abi?" He paused. "I've been trying to figure out what to do about everything Savannah's going through, and I'm thinking I'd benefit from a female perspective."

"I'd hoped to be in the pool for at least an hour," Isabella said, "so I have plenty of time."

"Trust me, I'd hoped you would be, too." He moved to the table and pulled out a chair for Isabella.

She couldn't recall Richard ever pulling out her chair; however, she did remember a time he reprimanded a waiter for neglecting to do so. "Thank you," she said, impressed with the gentlemanly gesture that came naturally to Titus.

The umbrella covering the table shaded his face, so she couldn't be certain, but it appeared his cheeks tinged a fraction as he said rather stiltedly, "You're welcome."

Isabella situated herself on the metal chair, taking a moment to tuck the top end of her towel securely at her chest and making sure as much of her skin as possible was covered. Water still dripped from her hair, but the warm afternoon air, combined with the thick terry towel, kept her from being too chilled as she waited to see what he wanted to talk about.

They sat for a moment, and Isabella tried to be patient as she eagerly anticipated Titus asking her advice. But his attention seemed to bounce between the barn, where Savannah stood near the fence rail petting Brownie, and the mountains, where the orange sun blazed vibrantly, with an occasional—and very quick—glance at Isabella in between.

Finally, unwilling to wait any longer, she cleared her throat. "You wanted to ask me something?"

This time, she was certain his cheeks turned a shade darker before he spoke.

"I'm sorry, Isabella. But it's been three years since I've even had a conversation with a woman." He shook his head, ran his hand through his hair.

Isabella watched as the dark strands fell messily around his chiseled face. He had such a strong presence, something that he didn't appear to realize, which made him even more appealing.

"I mean, I've spoken to women, but nothing much beyond a hello, or about the details of whatever I was building for them." One corner of his mouth kicked up in a half smile.

Isabella's heart melted a little more toward this compelling man, and as she waited for his attention to land on her again, she gave him a reassuring smile. "It's okay. I understand." Then, to help him out, she said, "If it's any consolation, I'm not used to a man wanting to hear my opinion about anything, so I may not be any more comfortable sitting here and answering your questions than you are sitting here and asking them."

Titus was so thrown by her statement that he forgot about being uncomfortable talking privately to a woman for the first time in three years. Isabella wasn't used to a man wanting to hear her opinion? Why not? What man had made her feel her views weren't worthy, and why hadn't Titus considered what might be going on in *her* world? He hadn't even thought about what had happened in her past to bring her here, to Claremont. She was such an intriguing, striking woman. Why would she have moved to a place this tiny? Was she trying to get away from the guy who didn't appreciate her?

"Who made you think your opinions didn't matter?"

She pushed a wet auburn lock of hair behind her ear and shifted in her seat. "I thought you wanted to ask me a question."

"I just did." Titus wasn't backing down

now. The thought of someone treating Isabella with anything less than the respect she deserved bothered him—a lot.

She pulled her towel tighter around her petite frame in an act that, whether she realized it or not, showed that she wanted protection. Titus could identify that now. He wondered how many clues that Isabella had been hurt he'd missed over the past two weeks.

"Did he hit you?" Titus asked.

Her grip on the towel tightened, eyes widened. "Oh, no. Never."

He believed her, and he was glad she hadn't been physically harmed, but he also knew that some guy hadn't treated her all that great, either. "So who was it?" Titus had been nervous about talking with Isabella, but now that the conversation was focused on her and on how someone could have done anything to hurt her, he wasn't nervous. On the contrary, he was engaged. And ready to make some man pay.

"My husband."

For the second time in two weeks, Titus felt sucker punched. Isabella was married? Well, of course she was. A woman as beautiful as Isabella, as kind and caring, would naturally have a husband. His attention moved to the bare ring finger on her left hand.

She followed where he stared and said, "My ex-husband, I should say. Our divorce was final six months ago. He tried for ten years to make me into what he wanted, and I let him—" she lifted slender shoulders "—but then he decided that wasn't enough." Her green eyes studied him as she added, "But it's okay. I'm happy now, getting a chance to start over. He started over, too."

"He's a fool."

Her soft laugh broke the tension. She straightened in her chair, gathered her hair and draped it over her right shoulder. "Thank you for that, but you'd probably like him if you met him. Most people do. He's a fairly popular guy, especially in his social circles."

Titus hardly heard her statement. His focus had fallen on her hands, maneuvering the long auburn waves that now curled past her shoulder. He wondered if her hair was as soft, as silky, as it appeared. Even now, still damp from her time in the pool, the red-brown ringlets caused him to wonder how they would feel in his hands, against his cheek or brushing against his lips.

And he again reminded himself that he had no business thinking about her that way, and that he didn't want to think of any woman that way—for a long, long time.

Her cheeks, he now noticed, had started to redden, and Titus realized with sudden clarity that he'd been caught staring and that he had no idea what she'd said. "I'm sorry," he said. "I wasn't listening."

She laughed again, and once more, he was drawn to the lyrical sound. "It doesn't matter. But you wanted to ask me something? About Savannah?"

Titus instinctively glanced toward the barn and saw his daughter leaning over the fence rail to timidly touch Brownie's nose. He got a grip on his infatuation with Isabella and refocused on the reason he'd asked her to talk. "I'm having a difficult time deciding what I can do to help her. I can't tell you how many articles and blogs I've read about telling her that her mom was dead, but none of them seemed right. So I kept putting it off until she finally asked me why I was so sad." He frowned. "I botched that one."

She leaned forward, reached a hand across the table and placed it on top of his. "Titus, I thought it was perfect that you waited. And her question gave you the opportunity not only to answer her, but to also see how Nan's death affected you."

For some reason, it felt odd hearing Isabella say Nan's name, but the touch of her hand comforted him to his very soul. He looked at her petite fingers and at the contrast of her creamy skin to his tan. Pale pink polish covered each nail and reminded him of another thing he'd forgotten.

"Savannah asked me to buy her fingernail polish," he said. "Probably three weeks ago."

"I have plenty of polish. I'll bring some tomorrow, and I'll paint her nails in the morning when I fix her hair."

"That'd be great," he said, still captured by the feel of her skin against his. Her thoughtfulness was never ending, as was her compassion for Savannah. And he believed she truly understood what Savannah was going through now, maybe even more than Titus. So he decided to ask her about what was bothering him most.

"The guy from the hospital who called last week to tell me about Nan..." he started. "He said that he found my name and number in some things she'd left behind, and that he would be boxing those up and mailing them to me soon. Of course, he thought I was her brother because apparently she'd given the hospital the impression that she was single." He didn't want to spend any time analyzing that with Isabella. "But maybe there are some keepsakes in there that she'd want her daughter—our daughter—to have."

"Are you wondering whether you should give them to Savannah now or wait until she's older?"

Titus shook his head. "No. I'm wondering if I want to even see what she left behind. I started to tell him not to bother mailing it."

"Because…" she prompted.

"She left us, Isabella. Walked out, leaving nothing but a note. I hate it that she got sick, that she died without us even knowing that she was in the hospital. But for some reason, she didn't want us to know. She didn't want to see me again, even when she knew that she was dying." He blew out a steady stream of air, closed his eyes and then opened them. "Don't you think that going through those things will only pour salt in the wound? And

I can't imagine it doing anything but hurting Savannah."

Isabella gently squeezed his hand. "Maybe there were things she wanted to tell you," she offered. "Or things she wanted to tell Savannah."

"She had three years to tell us anything she wanted." He shook his head. "I'll be honest. I don't want to go through her possessions. I'm done with the pain, done with the hurt. And I'm tired of seeing Savannah hurting because of Nan." He glanced at her hand, still resting on top of his. "So I wanted to ask someone who could look at this objectively, in particular a female, since I'm guessing you'd know more of what I should do for Savannah. Should I open that box when it comes?"

Isabella's throat pulsed as she swallowed. "I don't think I'm the one to answer that."

"But I'm asking you, and I want your answer."

"My answer is—" she let the word hang as she apparently considered the right thing to say "—that I think you should pray about it."

Definitely not the answer he wanted. Titus pulled his hand from hers and stood. "That's the thing. I'm done with that, too."

Chapter Five

❧

I didn't know how to tell you the truth...

Titus had just left his house and started toward Willow's Haven when his cell began to ring. He knew who was on the other end before looking at the screen on the truck's dashboard. Only one person called at 7:30 a.m.

Sure enough, *Mom* flashed back at him from the display.

He didn't have more than fifteen minutes before he would lose his signal when he reached Brodie and Savvy's property, but he didn't expect the conversation to take that long either. What could she say that she hadn't said before?

Glancing toward the backseat, he saw that Savannah was paying more attention to her doll than the ringing phone, but even so, he'd choose his words carefully, and he faded the sound to the front then turned the volume on the stereo system down to a minimum before answering. His parents had undoubtedly received the message he left for them last night, and now his mom wanted to try to make things better, the way moms do. Even though Titus would be thirty-one in a couple of months, she still wanted to fix things the way she had when he'd been Savannah's age.

Problem was, there was no way to make this better. Even so, he prepared to listen to her try and clicked the answer button on the steering wheel. "Hello."

"Oh, Titus," she said, her voice filled with sympathy. "Your dad and I got your message this morning. We didn't think to check the machine last night when we got home from church."

Titus should've thought of that. It'd been Wednesday night. Naturally, they would've been at church. A few weeks ago, so would he and Savannah. "I forgot it was Wednesday."

She inhaled, probably considering asking him why he hadn't been at a midweek service, too, but then she must've thought better of the idea, because she instead said, "We are so sorry to hear about Nan. You said she'd been sick?"

Savannah had started singing to Bessie. Titus was glad she was preoccupied so he could have this conversation without her hearing his mother's words.

"Kidney failure," he said, keeping his voice low just in case Savannah wasn't totally absorbed in the song. She knew that Nan was in heaven, and as far as Titus was concerned, that was plenty. She didn't need to know the details.

"Oh, my. How long had she been sick?"

"At least a year." The guy from the hospital had told him she'd been there for twelve months before she died. Titus had no idea where she'd been the two years before that, beyond working at the Y, and he assumed he'd never learn. All of his unanswered questions would remain unanswered, unless the package the hospital mailed held any insight into what had happened. And Titus still debated whether he wanted to see whatever was inside.

"Would you like for your father and I to come visit for a while?" she asked, obviously struggling with what to offer a son whose wife had abandoned him three years ago and then died without giving him or their daughter a chance to say goodbye.

Titus knew his parents would gladly make the six-hour drive from Orange Beach, on the southern border of the state, to stay with him, his father stepping in to help on the construction site and his mother cooking and taking care of Savannah. But eventually, they'd have to go home, and then he'd be hit with the reality of his life all over again. He'd just as soon deal with it head-on and get it over with. Plus, he didn't want to snap at his mother the way he'd snapped at Isabella last night. Which was why he was arriving at Willow's Haven a half hour earlier than usual. He wanted a chance to apologize first thing, as soon as she arrived and before the workday officially started. "I appreciate the offer, Mom, but we're doing okay."

"That's Granna?" Savannah piped up from the backseat. "Can I talk?"

He smiled, glad that his little girl had some form of a mother figure to look up to and also glad she hadn't been paying attention to the earlier portion of the conversation. "Savannah wants to talk to you, Mom." He turned up the volume and listened as Savannah told his mother about what was going on in her world, starting with the item that hurt the most.

"Hey, Granna," she said, "Mommy went to heaven."

"I know, dear."

Titus listened as his mom reminded Savannah about how heaven was a great place and that her mother would be happy there. He'd told her the same thing, as had Isabella and Savvy. He certainly hoped the knowledge gave her comfort.

"So, what are you doing today?" his mother asked, apparently to steer the conversation away from Nan.

"I'm going to work with Daddy, and Bessie's going with me."

"Is Bessie a friend of yours?"

Savannah released a little laugh. "No, she's not real. She's my doll."

"Do you like going to work with Daddy?" his mother asked, and Titus suspected it was to make sure she shouldn't drive up and save the day the way she'd offered. He held his breath and waited for his little girl to answer.

"Yes, ma'am. I like going to work with

Daddy, because Miss Isabella helps me fix Bessie's hair in the morning, so that her hair can be like mine. And then Miss Isabella fixes mine, too. Sometimes we do pigtails, but other times we do other things." She leaned forward. "Daddy, what's that thing Miss Isabella does, the fancy one I like?"

Titus was glad he remembered. "A French braid."

"Yes, that's it. Granna, it's a French braid."

Titus hadn't heard Savannah chat this easily with anyone, even his mom, in a very long time, since Nan had gone. And he suspected the change had everything to do with the little chats that had gradually turned into longer talks each morning with Isabella. His gratitude for her appearance in Savannah's life increased each time he realized what a profound impact she'd already had in her world. And he felt even worse about his abruptness with her yesterday afternoon. She'd only suggested that he pray to answer his problems. It wasn't her fault that praying was the last thing he wanted to do.

As if his mother knew his train of thought, she continued, "Miss Isabella. I don't think I've met her."

Titus could almost hear the wheels of her mind churning, wondering how Isabella fit into their world. "Is she nice?"

"Oh, yes, ma'am. She's very nice. She's going to teach me swimming, too, but right now I'm not so good."

"You'll get it, dear. Don't you worry."

Titus chanced another glance in the rear-view mirror to look at his little girl, nodding her head.

"I'm going to try again today."

"That's wonderful. Well, let me tell your daddy goodbye, sweetie. Granna loves you."

"I love you, too," Savannah said. "Daddy, did you hear? She wants to talk to you."

Titus dropped the volume again and asked Savannah, "Why don't you sing that song again to Bessie?"

"The song about the monkey?" she asked.

"That's the one," he said, though it didn't really matter what song she sang, as long as her attention wasn't on his conversation with his mother, because he suspected that she had a new subject to conquer.

After Savannah started singing about a curious monkey, he said, "Mom, I'll probably lose reception in a couple of minutes."

"Okay, dear. But before you go, I want to ask you something."

He could tell from her tone that this was going to be something that he might not want to hear. "Okay."

"How old is this Miss Isabella?"

He swallowed. "I haven't asked, but I'd guess late twenties."

"Pretty?"

Very. But he wouldn't walk into that trap. "Why do you ask?"

"So she is," she said. "You know, it sounds as though this Miss Isabella person is filling a void in Savannah's life."

Titus had been thinking the same thing, which made him even more frustrated with the way he'd ended their conversation yesterday. "I agree."

"I take it she's someone you've recently met? I don't recall anyone named Isabella when we've visited."

His mother never forgot a name or a face. "She just came to Claremont," he said, and he still wasn't quite sure why Isabella Gray had selected this tiny town.

"Right." She drew the word out, waited a beat and said what was on her mind, the way she always did. "Listen, I know you probably don't want to hear this. But maybe this Isabella could fill a void in your life, too."

Titus was suddenly glad that he was within a mile of Willow's Haven. He needed this conversation to end. "Mom, I just lost my—"

She cut him off. "No, Titus Elijah. You didn't *just* lose your wife. She left you and our granddaughter three years ago. And I'll be honest. Your father and I have been praying for someone to come into your life and bring you happiness again. You couldn't pursue that before because you didn't know what had happened to Nan and were still hopeful that she'd come back. And your daddy and I admire you for that. But you weren't meant to be alone, Titus. And Savannah wasn't meant to be without a mommy. It sounds like she's really taken with the new lady in town."

Titus turned onto the driveway leading to the trailer and was surprised that, of all times, his phone picked now to hold a signal longer than usual. "Yes, Mom, I think she is."

"I've often wondered if, sometimes, God doesn't use children to show us what's what," she said, and blissfully, her voice started breaking up.

"Mom, I'm losing the signal now. I'll call you back soon. Love you."

"Love you, too," she said, "but I still want to talk about…"

The display blinked, and the signal was gone.

Titus heaved a big sigh, glad that the first uncomfortable conversation of the morning was over. Then he looked ahead to see that Isabella's car wasn't yet parked at the trailer. Good. That'd give him a little time to prepare for uncomfortable conversation number two.

After Titus's brusque departure yesterday afternoon, Isabella didn't expect him to want to speak to her this morning. In fact, she suspected that he'd probably bring Savannah early, before she arrived, so that he wouldn't have to see Isabella before he started working. That's what Richard would've done. If Isabella ever said or did anything that disappointed him, he'd ignore her until *she* ended up apologizing, often when she couldn't even remember what she'd done to earn his disappointment.

So she was surprised when she neared the trailer to see that Titus *had* arrived early but hadn't started working. And definitely wasn't ignoring her. In fact, he lounged on the front steps, his elbows resting on the top step and his long legs, encased in well-worn jeans, stretched out in front of him as he watched her park her car.

The sleeves on his navy work shirt were rolled up, exposing tan forearms while also emphasizing sturdy biceps hidden beneath the fabric. A breeze played with his hair, and the morning sunlight seemed to showcase his eyes, lifting the flecks of gold from the brown and green.

Riveted by the image before her, Isabella forgot to put the car in Park and slammed her foot on the brake when it moved too close to the trailer. And, scarily, too close to the man sitting on the deck. She stopped mere inches away from Titus and knocked over a pile of firewood. Logs went rolling everywhere.

But Isabella wasn't concerned about the wood. Have mercy, she could have hit Titus.

He'd jumped out of the way in the nick of time, and his wide eyes and tilted head said she'd probably caused a nice surge of adrenaline to kick in. Embarrassed, she shrugged and attempted to act as though she wasn't sure how it happened. Truthfully, she knew exactly what happened. She was captivated, once again, by Nan's husband.

She'd worked very hard throughout yesterday and last night to remind herself to think of Titus that way. As Nan's. Because he obviously still had a hard time thinking of himself in any other light. Why else would he find it so difficult to open the box of her things that the hospital would send? He didn't want their marriage to be over, even though he hadn't seen her in three years. Even now, with the news that she'd passed on, he still felt committed to Nan. And Isabella understood. She'd loved Nan, too, and she still missed the friendship they shared, even if Nan hadn't been completely honest.

But why was Titus apparently waiting for Isabella now, after he'd been so short with her when she'd suggested he pray for answers?

Only one way to find out.

Grabbing her purse, she climbed from the car and took a step toward him, but her heel caught on the hem of her skirt, and she ended up tripping forward almost as suddenly as her car had stopped. One hand still clutched the strap of her purse, and the other reached forward expecting to hit the ground. But everything came to a halt when she found herself in those strong arms she'd admired a moment ago.

"Hey," he said, his voice a deep rumble as his woodsy, masculine scent once again teased her senses. "Are you okay?"

No, her mind whispered, *I'm still falling, and I don't want to fall for any man again, even you—especially you—you're Nan's ex.* But then she harnessed the truth and answered, "Yes, I'm okay. Just clumsy." She reached forward to free her shoe from the skirt and noticed that he still held her, balancing her in case she did actually drop into a pile of mush at his feet. Feeling her cheeks grow warm, she straightened and took the slight step necessary to reluctantly ease her way out of his embrace. "Thanks. I'm not sure what happened."

"I'd guess you've got a rush of adrenaline causing a bit of shock," he said smoothly, soothingly, as though *she* was the one who'd nearly been hit, and when Isabella raised her eyebrow at his quick assessment, he explained, "Happens to me every now and then, usually when I lose my footing on a roof, or when I drop a nail gun, or—" he grinned "—when I nearly get hit by a car."

"I am so sorry."

"Actually, that's why I'm here," he said. "To tell you I'm sorry."

Isabella took a wobbly step and realized that it wasn't merely her skirt that had caused her loss of footing and that he was probably right. Her knees felt like jelly, as though she was suffering from that adrenaline rush he mentioned. But she wasn't certain whether it'd come from the near miss of the car or the near proximity of the man.

He saw her falter and wrapped an arm around her again. "Here, let me help you to the deck. You spook kinda easily, don't ya?"

"I guess so." How would she ever get a grip on her heart around him? Isabella couldn't help but compare the way he treated her to the way Richard had. Richard would have seen her stumble as a sign of weakness, of something that she should work on and gain control of, but Titus saw it as an opportunity to offer her support.

She could get used to being treated like this.

He'd started leading her to one of the deck

chairs, but then Isabella noticed the wood that had once been a neat stack beside a fire pit and now looked like someone had vandalized the place.

"I need to clean that up before Savvy gets here," she said. "And I should back the car up to the right spot." She hadn't even thought to put the thing in Reverse and get it away from the deck. Isabella was embarrassed that she'd been so preoccupied and certainly didn't want to explain what had held her attention at the time.

"I'll pick it up," he said, stepping toward the wayward wood. "I'm dressed for it. You're not." He indicated her skirt and heels.

But she wasn't about to let Titus clean this up on his own. "I can work in this." To prove it, she lifted a log and placed it where the stack had been.

He picked up two of them and put them beside her single one, then continued stacking them up two or three at a time, while Isabella focused on helping...instead of noticing how easily he handled the heavy logs. "I haven't seen this side of you yet," he said, putting three more logs on the pile.

"What side?" she asked, adding another one.

"The stubborn side."

She glanced up to see him smiling. "I'm not stubborn," she clarified. "I just don't expect someone else to clean up my mess."

They'd both ended up at the stack at the same time, and he resituated the logs to keep them steady, then paused. "There's a reason for that, right? Something to do with your ex?"

She showed him her palms, covered with wood bark that flaked away each time she picked up a log. "He wouldn't have been willing to get his hands dirty."

One eyebrow lifted, and Titus smirked. "Some guys are like that," he said. "Typically, it's the ones with a lot of money in the bank."

"Money isn't everything." Richard's money had never been important to her. She'd simply wanted him to love her the way she was, without feeling the need to change her into what he wanted her to be.

"It isn't everything," he agreed, "but it does help." Titus grabbed the last of the logs. "When Nan left, the construction industry had hit an all-time low. And I'd spent what cash we had on the truck because I had actually thought that business would be picking up when it headed south." He put the logs on the top of the stack. "I didn't know how we were going to make it through the year financially, and I'd told her that the week before."

Isabella didn't know why Nan left, but she couldn't believe it had anything to do with money. "You think that's why she left?" she asked.

He dusted the wood shavings from his hands and shrugged. "I'll never know now."

Her heart ached for him, the sensitive man who still cared about why his wife had left him and his little girl. And recalling his sensitivity reminded her of what he'd said earlier. She also dusted the wood from her hands, then smoothed her palms over the top of her skirt and asked, "Why did you need to tell me you're sorry?"

He glanced toward the wooded area surrounding the trailer. "Basically, because I was a first-class jerk yesterday," he said. "I asked your advice, and you gave it. But when it wasn't what I wanted to hear, I cut you off. And that was wrong." Then he brought his gaze back to her, and once more she was caught off guard by the sincerity in his eyes.

Richard had never been so honest with Isabella. Or cared whether he hurt her feelings.

"It's okay," she said.

He shook his head. "No, Isabella, it isn't. I shouldn't have talked to you that way, and I'm sorry."

Still shocked at a man apologizing, she simply stared.

"Now's the time where you tell me you forgive me," he said, and his mouth slid into a grin.

"Oh, my. I'm sorry," she said.

Titus didn't know why she found it so hard to admit that he'd treated her wrong, but he wasn't about to let himself off the hook. He'd acted like a jerk, and he was sorry. But somehow, *she'd* ended up apologizing.

He wouldn't have any part of that. "No, that's what *I* said. *I'm* sorry. Your line is, 'Titus, I forgive you.'"

She laughed, the response he'd hoped for, because he truly loved hearing Isabella laugh. She finally said, "Titus, I forgive you."

He smiled. "Thanks." He probably should've accepted her apology and moved away from her, because they'd ended up very close, both of them leaning against the deck near the firewood as they spoke. But he didn't want to.

He looked at her for a moment while he gathered the right words and was momentarily captured by the image of the woman before him. She wore a turquoise blouse and long floral skirt that emphasized her femininity, as did the way she had her auburn waves pulled back in some kind of loose twist that he was certain Savannah would want her to try with her hair. A couple of long curls had escaped when they'd restacked the wood, and that only added to her appeal. And as usual, she wore minimal makeup, a hint of gloss on her lips, a shimmery shadow that highlighted the deep green of her eyes and a little mascara. But he also noticed something he hadn't seen before, a faint spray of freckles on her nose and cheeks.

"Was there something else?" she asked, her voice trembling a little.

Titus had probably made her uncomfortable by blatantly staring—again. It really had been too long since he'd spent this much time with a female. He cleared his throat. "Yes," he said. "I wanted to explain what happened yesterday, when you suggested I pray. The truth is, a few weeks ago I wouldn't have had a problem praying for guidance with how to help Savannah, or whether to go through Nan's things, or anything else. But ever since that phone call from the hospital, and after three years of constantly praying for a different ending to all of this, I guess I didn't see the need." The honesty of his statement, and the fact that he'd shared it with Isabella, surprised him, even if it was exactly how he felt. Nan had abandoned him, and then God followed suit.

Not knowing what she'd think of his statement, he looked away from Isabella and toward the cleared area, the sites for the first two cabins. He thought about what he planned to do today with regard to the next wooded area and about the men he needed to call to begin setting up the subcontractors he'd hire once he was ready to break ground. Anything to keep his mind off the woman to whom he'd just confessed that he was losing his faith.

The touch of warm fingers on his hand forced him to turn back to her, and the compassion in her eyes said she didn't judge him. "It's easier to let Him help than to blame Him. Trust me, I know."

Each time she spoke, Titus realized how very much he didn't know about Isabella Gray and how much he'd like to know more. "Are you talking about your marriage?"

"No, though God did get me through those years, too," she said. "But I'm talking about the years before my marriage." She took a deep breath and glanced at the trailer. "See, there's a reason I'm so happy being here, helping with the start-up of Willow's Haven."

Her hand still touched his, and he felt a slight tremble in it as she spoke. "What reason?"

She looked back to Titus, and he saw her eyes were moist. "Growing up, I prayed for a place like this." She blinked a couple of times, and those tears fell free. She moved her hand from Titus's and swiped at her cheeks. "I was trying not to cry," she whispered.

Titus didn't know what to say or do. But he had the strongest urge to take her in his arms and hold her, make her understand that he'd protect her, because he had that desire, too, to protect Isabella Gray from whatever caused her to cry. But that wasn't the right thing. He'd just lost his wife, and he was no-where near the point where he could hold another woman in his arms, even to provide comfort. So he stood his ground and waited for her to continue.

"My mother abandoned me when I was born," she said softly.

Her statement hit him like a punch to the gut. Isabella had been abandoned? "I'm so sorry."

She shook her head. "No, that wasn't the bad part. I can't remember anything about her letting me go, of course," she said, attempting a watery smile. "But the years after..." She paused, looked up for a moment. "I spent eighteen years in orphanages and a few foster homes, but never anything permanent. And never anything that felt like a real home. Nothing that felt safe." She shivered. "Or even clean. I often went to bed hungry and never felt I could do anything right."

His chest tugged, throat closing in at the thought of Isabella, abandoned and mistreated. Again, that urge to protect her burned through him and he repeated, "I'm so sorry."

She took a quick breath of air. "I'm okay."

Titus instantly recalled how often she made similar statements. "It's okay...I'm okay..." He wondered if that was her way of dealing with the pain, by telling herself that it was all right. But it wasn't all right. No one should be raised like that. No child should feel unloved.

"But during those years, God got me through," she said. "I didn't know all that much about Him, because not many of the places I stayed went to church on a regular basis, or even had Bibles. So when I did get a glimpse of Him, I'd grab on for dear life. And I'd pray."

Her advice telling him to pray took on an entirely new meaning, and Titus felt even more like a heel for being abrupt. "Isabella, I'm sorry for being so rude yesterday afternoon. I had no idea what you'd been through, and I shouldn't have dismissed your advice." He felt terrible for being so crude. "Please, forgive me."

Her mouth lifted, and he was glad to see her eyes light up as she answered, "I already did, remember?"

"Hey, Miss Isabella's here!"

Titus turned toward Savannah's voice and saw that she, Rose and Daisy had started down the hill from Brodie and Savvy's cabin. He could hear her excitement at seeing the lady she'd grown so close to already, and it warmed his heart even more, because Isabella had touched his heart thoroughly.

"I wondered if they were in the trailer," Isabella said.

"I took Savannah to the house so you and I could talk," he explained, "and Savvy was baking cinnamon rolls for the girls to share."

Isabella nodded, then quickly asked, "Can you tell I've been crying?"

He looked at her face, the freckles a little more copper due to her emotion and her eyes still glistening from her tears. A hint of mascara showed beneath each eye, and he took his thumb and tenderly wiped the smudges away. "Not now," he said.

"Thank you."

Savannah reached the porch first, and Titus was pleased to see the contrast in his little girl. Two weeks ago, she'd rarely walked with her head up, much less run ahead of the twins in her eagerness to get anywhere. But she'd run now, not to see Titus but to be near Isabella.

"Miss Isabella, did you bring it?" she asked excitedly.

Isabella gave his daughter a full smile, all hints of sadness disappearing in her desire to care for his daughter. She opened her purse and withdrew three bottles of fingernail polish. "I brought a few colors, so you all can choose what you like the best."

Savannah, Rose and Daisy clapped their enthusiasm, while Titus heard his mother's words from earlier.

It sounds as though this Miss Isabella person is filling a void in Savannah's life.

And then...

Maybe this Isabella could fill a void in your life, too.

Chapter Six

And I didn't want to lie.

Sparkly pink nail polish. *That's* what finally got Savannah to ease onto the top step in the pool.

Titus watched as Isabella, sitting beside Savannah, placed her hand back in the water. "See if yours looks like this, too," she said to Savannah.

Savannah peered at her mentor's hand and then placed her own fingers next to Isabella's beneath the water's surface. "It does sparkle more in the water." She lifted her foot to see her toes shimmering, too, thanks to Isabella painting all toes and fingers this morning. Smiling brighter than Titus had seen her smile in weeks, maybe even years, she turned to him. "Daddy, come look at it sparkle!"

Titus moved toward the pair in the pool and decided he wasn't sure who was smiling brighter, Savannah or Isabella.

Savannah put both hands in the water and tilted them back and forth to allow the glittery polish to catch the sunlight. "See? Isn't it pretty?"

"Beautiful," he said, but he wasn't merely talking about the sparkling nails. The image of Savannah happy, combined with the undeniable compassion glowing on Isabella's face, warmed his heart in places that, until the past couple of days, had been iced over for three years.

"So what do you think? Would you want to go out a little way from the step, if you were holding on to me?" Isabella asked, her voice filled with tenderness.

Savannah's smile slipped a little. "I don't know. Can I touch the bottom there?"

"We would stay in the shallow part, where you can touch," Isabella promised. "But we don't have to move from the step today if you don't want to. We can wait."

Savannah glanced toward Titus. "I want to, but I want Daddy to come in the water, too."

Titus should've considered that, but he honestly hadn't anticipated her getting in the pool today. "Oh, honey, I didn't bring a swimsuit." He'd changed out of his long-sleeved work shirt into a T-shirt, but still wore old jeans and boots. Not exactly swimming attire.

"You could sit on the side and watch me. And maybe put your feet in," Savannah said. "It isn't too scary."

Until today, she'd seen everything about this pool as scary, but thanks to Isabella—and a bottle of sparkly fingernail polish—that fear was slowly but surely evaporating. "That's a good idea." He sat on the concrete near the girls, removed one boot and then the other while they watched, and then followed suit with his socks. He stuffed the socks in the boots and rolled up his jeans to his calves, while Savannah clapped her approval and Isabella smiled hers.

Sliding his feet into the water, he made a show of hissing as if it were too cold. Savannah giggled and Isabella winked at him. Titus laughed, the surprising gesture from Isabella making him feel as happy as the unrestrained giggle from his little girl.

Isabella eased away from the step. She dipped to her shoulders, then stood and moved her hands around in the water. "See," she said to Savannah. "It isn't deep at all here."

Savannah nodded but made no effort to move off of the step. Titus could tell Isabella was intent on taking this slow, encouraging Savannah without pushing her. He nodded his approval, and she gave him another of those easy smiles.

While Savannah garnered her courage and Isabella continued gently circling her hands along the top of the water, Titus found himself appreciating Isabella's beauty even more. Her auburn waves appeared more chestnut than red when wet, giving her an almost exotic appearance as she stood in the water. She wore a modest green one-piece, similar to the suits she'd worn every other day. There wasn't anything too revealing about it, but even so, any male would have a difficult time not noticing how fit she looked, her petite features accentuating the femininity of the woman who'd drifted through his thoughts ever since she arrived in town. And stayed there continually since their conversation yesterday.

Over the past two weeks, he'd learned a few things about Isabella Gray. She'd had a husband who didn't appreciate her, and she'd been raised without being loved. Now, as he watched her ease her fingertips toward his little girl and then saw Savannah slide her fingers to intertwine with Isabella's, Titus was overwhelmed with gratitude. And though he did know a few things about her, he wanted very much to know more. It wasn't as if he wanted anything romantic. He knew he wasn't ready for that, not after what had happened with Nan. But he was very interested in her because of how she affected Savannah. That was it. Really.

"Look at me, Daddy!" Savannah had left the step and was letting Isabella guide her around the water. They weren't actually doing anything like swimming, but she was in the water, and he saw no sign of fear, because Isabella wasn't leaving her side.

His throat tightened. "Yes, look at you." Titus didn't miss the similarity in what was going on in the pool and what had happened in Savannah's life. Nan had left Savannah, and his little girl had probably felt as if she'd been tossed into the deep with no way out, no mother to help, certain to drown. But Isabella, understanding that feeling from her own experience, had taken her time with Savannah, staying there and encouraging her as she worked through the fear.

He saw Isabella catch his gaze, concern covering her features as though she knew what he was thinking. And maybe she did. Then he saw her gather Savannah in her arms and whisper something in her ear that made Savannah look at him and smile.

Titus, not knowing what else to do, returned the gesture.

And then he saw the flash of mischievousness on Isabella's face as she slowly brought Savannah closer to her father…and they began splashing him mercilessly.

Titus was so stunned that it took him a moment to react, but within seconds, he began kicking playful waves in his own wet attack—nothing too big as to frighten Savannah but enough that he could join in the fun.

The squeals of laughter from the woman and the child were infectious, and pretty soon, he was laughing nearly as hard and was almost as wet as the two in the pool.

"Okay, okay," he finally said, holding up his hands in defense. "Mercy."

Isabella and Savannah stopped their assault and, still laughing, made a few more turns around the shallow end of the pool before they decided to call it a successful day.

Within minutes, they'd dried off and put T-shirts and shorts over their suits. Savannah couldn't seem to stop grinning, and Titus couldn't either.

"Daddy, can we go get ice cream?" Savannah saw a trip to the Sweet Stop, the candy and ice-cream store on the town square, as the ultimate form of celebration. Titus agreed that this afternoon's accomplishment in the pool was definitely worth celebrating.

"Sure," he said, and her smile got even bigger, pushing into her cheeks.

"Can I go ask Abi if she wants to come?"

He glanced toward the barn to see Abi with her parents, Landon and Georgiana Cutter. "Of course," he said.

Savannah didn't miss a beat. "And Miss Isabella can come, too?"

Isabella shook her head. "Oh, no, you don't have to..."

But Titus didn't waver. "Of course," he repeated to Savannah. To Isabella, he added, "Please. Savannah wants you to come." When she opened her mouth to apparently protest again, he added, "And so do I."

She nodded. "Okay."

Savannah rushed toward him and hugged him. "Thank you, Daddy." Then she moved to Isabella and wrapped both arms around her in a hug, making no effort to let go.

"Thank you, Miss Isabella."

Isabella ran her hand down Savannah's hair and visibly swallowed. "You're welcome, sweetie. We'll do it again tomorrow, okay?"

Savannah nodded. "Okay."

Titus waited for her to release Isabella from the hug, but she continued holding on, and for a moment he thought his little girl might be crying. His heart couldn't take seeing her cry, for any reason, happy or sad. Then he realized what had her so absorbed in the hug.

"Miss Isabella," she whispered, "I love you."

Emotion fisted around Titus's heart and held tight as he watched Isabella's tears slip free. She tried to casually brush them away and Savannah, with her face still pushed against Isabella's side, didn't seem to notice. But Titus did. And he also noticed the undeniable honesty delivered in her response.

"Oh, Savannah, I love you, too."

Isabella hadn't been able to say anything to Titus after Savannah left to get Abi. The little girl's sweet confession had overwhelmed her to the point that she simply couldn't speak, and she could barely look at him as she gathered her things at the pool. Thankfully, she'd driven her car to the Cutter ranch and was now following them to the square. She needed this time alone to work through the surplus of emotions that the afternoon had stirred in her soul.

But the fifteen-minute drive to the square wasn't long enough. In fact, the only thing she managed to do during its duration was continue to remember how it felt to be there, with Titus and Savannah, playing in the pool and laughing, seeing him look at her with such thankfulness for helping his little girl and then hearing Savannah say the sweetest words she'd ever heard.

By the time they pulled into the parking spaces at the back of the Sweet Stop, Isabella had shed so many tears that her neck was damp. She dropped her visor and glanced at her reflection in the mirror to check the damage. As she feared, she was a mess. Her hair, naturally wavy, went a little on the troll doll side after a visit to the pool. Normally, she'd pull it into a ponytail, but she'd forgotten to bring a hairband. And she certainly hadn't expected an invitation to go out for ice cream with Titus, Savannah and Abi.

Makeup was nonexistent, as it always was after she went swimming, except for a blur of smudged mascara beneath each eye. And a hint of it on her cheeks from where it must have slid south at some point in her crying spell.

Thankful that there hadn't been two parking spaces side by side, she patted her cheeks and attempted to smooth her hair while Titus parked a short distance away. She was still trying to make herself look a little more presentable when he opened her door.

"Hey, it's easier to eat the ice cream if we go inside the shop," he said, giving her a smile that warmed her heart.

Then he apparently noticed her eyes, or her makeup, or maybe her hair, because his features warmed and he asked, "Are you going to be okay?"

He crouched down beside her, and Isabella focused on regaining control, sniffing, taking a deep breath…and then remembering that the girls were with him. She peered around him. "Where are Savannah and Abi?"

"Abi's uncle John and aunt Dana were entering the Sweet Stop when we drove up, so the girls went on in with them," he said.

Grateful they hadn't seen her upset, she reached for her purse and withdrew a tissue, then used the mirror to attempt a better job of cleaning away the smudges. "I'm better now," she said, wadding up the tissue. "Sorry for the tears. Let's go get that ice cream."

His arm propped on the edge of the car, and he was close enough that she could smell his woodsy cologne. Or maybe that was simply the way he smelled. Either way, she liked it, and she found herself inhaling deeply just to appreciate it, while she waited for him to ease back and let her get out of the car.

But he didn't budge and, instead, continued filling the space from the open door.

"Isabella, I can tell you're used to apologizing for things, even things you can't control. You don't need to feel badly for being upset. But I do want you to tell me what's wrong. Maybe I can help."

She could tell he wasn't moving until she answered, and again memories of the past ten years with Richard resurfaced. With her ex-husband, if she apologized, he'd merely accept the apology and they'd move along. He didn't care what was wrong—he simply wanted her to dry it up and get over it. But Titus cared. She could hear it in his tone, sense it in the way he looked at her now. "It's just that I've never had that happen before, and I guess it really hit me how wonderful it feels."

He eased back from the car a little and studied her. "You helped children who were afraid of the water in Atlanta, too. How was helping Savannah different?" But even as he asked her, she could tell that he suspected how very different it was. Everything about Savannah was different, because she reminded Isabella of herself and because she was the daughter Nan had never mentioned… and because she belonged to Titus.

But none of those things were what Isabella referred to now. "That isn't what I'm talking about."

"Then what is?" he asked.

"I've never had a child...tell me that she loved me."

He hesitated, and she noticed his jaw flex before he spoke. She wondered if she'd told him too much. She didn't want him feeling sorry for her, but he'd said he wanted to know why she was upset, and Isabella didn't want to lie to Titus. Ever.

Then she remembered the reason she had come to Claremont and that she had essentially lied, or at least withheld the truth, when she didn't tell him about Nan.

Isabella swallowed, thought about the misconception and decided she needed to tell him everything. Right here, right now. "Titus, I'm sorry..."

"No," he said. "I won't let you apologize for earning a place in Savannah's heart. I'll admit that it surprised me when she told you that she loved you, but not in a bad way. Not at all. It means the world to me that she has found someone to trust again, someone to love. I know that she loves me, trusts me, but

Nan leaving her really seemed to put a hold on her ability to have those types of emotions with anyone else. But ever since you came…" He took a deep breath, let it out. "Well, I want you to know that when Savannah says something, especially something like that, she means it. And I also want to thank you for giving her the confidence to love again."

Isabella couldn't ruin this moment by telling him about Nan. He was as touched by Savannah's words as she'd been, and that realization nearly pushed her tears free again.

"Oh no, you don't," he said. "No more tears, or the girls will think I made you cry." Then he stood and held out a hand. "Come on. You need ice cream. The Sweet Stop makes an amazing mint chocolate chip. What do you say?"

Isabella put her hand in his and climbed out of the car. "That sounds perfect."

Chapter Seven

I wanted to be a good wife.

Titus barely tasted the ice cream, so consuming were his thoughts on everything that had happened this afternoon. He'd been taken aback with Savannah's honest admission, even more with Isabella's response to it and the fact that she'd never heard a child confess love. He wanted to talk to her more about her past and her reasons for coming to Claremont, but she was still recovering from the emotional pull of Savannah's words. And right now wasn't the time for a private conversation. Their table was full of happy ice cream eaters.

John and Dana Cutter sat across from Titus and Isabella at a red round table while their one-year-old son, Jacob, sat in a high chair by Dana. Savannah and Abi had selected a colorful kid-sized table by the window.

Titus watched as Savannah, wide-eyed and excited, told Abi again about how she went in the pool. Although Abi was three years older than his little girl, she hung on every word and told Savannah what a wonderful job she was doing, which caused Savannah's smile to grow even bigger. They chatted nonstop while they worked on their ice-cream cones, and Titus marveled at the difference the past two weeks had made in Savannah.

Isabella had unquestionably been the primary cause of Savannah's new disposition, and he wasn't the only one who'd noticed.

"I saw Savannah in the pool with you today," Dana said to Isabella. "I have to admit that it gave me goose bumps to see her enjoying herself like that." Then she paused and looked at Titus. "I don't mean that she hasn't been happy before, necessarily, it's just that…" Her voice fell off, and she looked to her husband for help.

"I think Titus knows what you meant," John said.

Titus nodded. "I do, and I feel the same

way. She's been through a tough few years. We both have, and the whole town knows it." Savannah's laugh trickled through the air when she accidentally got ice cream on her nose. Titus watched her wipe it away, pure joy seeping into his soul. "But she's finding her way out of the sadness now." He debated whether to give credit where credit was due, since he didn't want to embarrass Isabella, but the truth was the truth, and he'd say it. "And a big part of that is because of Isabella."

She held up a palm. "Oh, I just tried to help."

"You're amazing with her," Dana said, giving Jacob a spoonful of chocolate ice cream. "And Savvy told me how excited she is to have you working at Willow's Haven. She said you're a natural with children."

"I love being a part of Willow's Haven, and I do love children." Isabella watched Jacob clap his delight as Dana fed him yet another spoonful of the cold treat, and Titus didn't miss the look of longing. He'd seen it in Nan's eyes, before they had Savannah. The look of a woman who wanted a child of her own.

Isabella had mentioned that she'd been married for ten years. Now Titus wondered why she and her husband didn't have children. So many things about her had piqued his curiosity, and he wanted to spend more time with her to learn the answers to his questions.

"Daddy?"

Titus turned toward Savannah and saw that she and Abi had finished their cones and stood near the door leading to the square. "Yes?"

"Abi said her uncle John and aunt Dana are taking her to the toy store now. Can I go, too?"

"I'm not buying anything today," Abi explained. "I'm just picking things out for my birthday."

"Her birthday is still a month away," John said, grinning, "but our Abi is a planner."

Dana laughed. "And she knows her uncle John can't say no to her."

"As if her aunt Dana can," John countered.

Dana laughed as she wiped excess ice cream off Jacob's face and then eased him out of the high chair and into her lap. "Okay. Guilty as charged."

John and Dana had finished their cones, but Titus and Isabella had hardly started on theirs, since they'd spent that extra time in the parking lot before entering.

Dana apparently noticed and said, "If it's okay with y'all, Savannah can go with us to the toy store while you finish eating, and then we'll bring her back here."

Titus had spied the traditional bags of day-old bread near the counter and had an idea to give him a little time to talk to Isabella. "That sounds great," he said. "But why don't y'all meet us by the fountain? We'll go out there and feed the geese after we finish our ice cream."

Isabella looked surprised but didn't say no to spending more time with him.

"Okay," John said. "So it looks like we're heading to the Tiny Tots Treasure Box."

"My favorite place!" Abi darted ahead, with Savannah at her heels.

"Thanks for letting her tag along," Titus said to the pair.

"We're happy to have her." Dana shifted Jacob from one hip to the other. "And so happy to see her smiling again."

"Me, too," he admitted.

After they'd taken the kids out of the shop,

Isabella said, "You're blessed to have such amazing friends here."

Although he was certain she hadn't meant to, she'd given him another glimpse of what she'd missed in the past. Friendship. "That's the beauty of small-town living. Everybody knows everyone." He'd finished the top of his ice cream and took a bite from the cone. "Occasionally it isn't such a great thing, but most of the time, you appreciate it."

She peered at him as she nibbled at her cone, waited a moment and then softly spoke what was on her mind. "I'm guessing it was hard after Nan left, with everyone knowing what had happened. Do you think it was worse because you live in a small town?"

From some people, the question would've seemed nosy, but not from Isabella. He could tell by her tone and the undeniable concern on her face that she realized how hard it was living in a town that knew his wife had abandoned him and Savannah. "I think it was worse living in a place this size," he said. "It'd have been different if it were only adults looking at us that way and saying things, but even the kids know what's going on around town."

"The kids?"

He remembered that Monday in May when he'd picked Savannah up from school to find her eyes red and watery. "On the day after Mother's Day, some kids on the playground at school asked Savannah why she didn't have a mommy."

"Oh, Titus, what did she say?"

"She told me that she said that she did have a mommy but that she was just not here right now. Then she asked me why she wasn't." He looked out the window to view all of the people on the square, anything to keep from watching Isabella's solemn expression while his emotions attempted to get the best of him. Finally, he glanced back at her and said, "I wanted to give her a decent answer, but I didn't have anything to offer but the truth." He shrugged. "I told her I didn't know."

"I'm sorry you had to go through that."

"It wouldn't have been so difficult if Savannah hadn't had to go through it, too. That was the tough part—going out, to town or to church or wherever, and seeing people look at her that way, as if they were so sorry for her. It tore my heart out."

"They didn't realize how blessed she was," Isabella said. Her cone had started to melt, and she took another small bite to stop its progress. "Savannah had you. So many children don't have anyone, ever. But even when she lost her mom, she still had you there, loving her, caring for her…showing her that all people don't leave."

"Thank you for saying that." A few people over the past three years had made similar statements, but none of them could relate to Savannah the way Isabella could. She'd been abandoned. She knew what it felt like to have no one to love her, care for her, show her that all people don't leave. Maybe that was the reason Titus's chest clenched and he had the strongest urge to show Isabella that someone could be there for her, too.

She stopped eating, grabbed a couple of napkins from the dispenser in the center of the table and wrapped the remainder of her cone inside. "I can't eat another bite," she said.

Titus considered that the topic of conversation may have affected her appetite, so he decided to lighten the mood. He tossed the end of his cone in his mouth, chewed and swallowed. "Me, either. Can't eat another bite."

Thankfully, she laughed, which was exactly what he'd wanted. Then he noticed a small dot from a chocolate chip near the corner of her mouth and pointed to his own. "You have a little chocolate, right here."

"Oh." She swiped the opposite side with a napkin.

He leaned forward, touched his finger to the spot and tenderly wiped it away. "I got it."

She blinked, visibly swallowed, and the tight rein he'd put on his heart slipped a little. "Thanks."

"You're welcome." He looked up to see Jasmine Waddell, the blond college student who worked behind the counter, staring at them with her mouth open. Titus could almost hear the roots of the gossip vine taking hold and preparing to thrive. He cleared his throat. "I'll go buy some of the bread bits so we can feed the geese." Then he stood, grabbed one of the brown bags of bread from the huge basket by the counter and went to make his purchase from Jasmine.

"That's Isabella," she said, ringing him up. "I met her at church Sunday. She's from Atlanta and is working at the new place that Brodie and Savvy are building for orphan kids. Willow's Haven."

Amazing, the short bio for Isabella that had already made its way around Claremont. Obviously the gossip vine was still alive and well, probably courtesy of RuthEllen Riley at the Cut and Curl and Jasmine, undoubtedly privy to every conversation that occurred at the Sweet Stop. "That's right." Titus handed her the cash for the bread.

"So she's helping Savannah learn to swim?" she asked, placing the bills in the cash register while authenticating Titus's suspicion that she'd been eavesdropping.

"She is."

"That's awesome," Jasmine continued, counting out the change while blissfully unaware of the disapproval in Titus's tone. "She's very pretty."

To argue would be useless, not to mention an outright lie. "Yes, she is," he agreed.

"You should date her." This was delivered almost as a command, and he turned to see if Isabella had heard the girl's directive words.

Jasmine started laughing, the type of giggle common with girls her age. It reminded Titus of the way Nan used to laugh when they'd first met, and it made him wonder what Isabella sounded like when she laughed that way.

"Don't worry. She walked over to the door," Jasmine said. "She didn't hear me." Then she dropped his change in his open palm. "But you should. Date her, I mean."

"I'll keep that in mind," he said, slipping the change in his pocket. He picked up the bag and moved toward the door, then opened it for Isabella. But Jasmine, apparently deciding since she was already offering sage advice she might as well keep it up, yelled, "And you should come back to church, too!"

He winced then answered, "I'll keep that in mind, as well." Then he waited for Isabella to exit and left the ice cream shop…and the employee who was too young to realize she should keep some opinions to herself.

They walked toward the three-tiered fountain in the middle of the square with Titus reflecting on Jasmine's unfiltered guidance. Knowing Isabella had heard the last statement, he asked, "You think she's right, don't you?"

She slowed, which caused Titus to look her way as she spoke. "I wasn't going to say anything, but, yes, I do."

Grateful that she hadn't chosen the girl's statement as an opportunity to gently reprimand him, he confided, "Savannah actually asked me why we didn't go to church this week. The truth is I don't feel right going when I'm so angry." He didn't have to add that he was angry at God. He was certain she knew.

She continued walking slowly and took a moment before she responded. Then she inhaled and said, "It may seem harder, but it's actually much easier to deal with the pain and disappointment if you let Him help. But I can understand how it'd be tempting to get angry with Him after everything you've been through. You want to blame someone for what Nan did, walking out on y'all, and you want to blame someone for her death. And He seems like the best target. Since He is the place where the buck stops, so to speak."

Titus couldn't deny her sincere assessment. She'd nailed it. "You never got angry with Him? With everything you went through growing up? At all of those orphanages and foster homes you told me about?"

Her mouth lifted in a slight smile. "I couldn't," she said. "I needed God too much to get mad at Him. Most of the time, the only positive things I had to cling to were the tiny snippets that I'd learned about Him on those rare visits to church. I knew that He loved me, even when it seemed no one else ever would. I needed to know that. I think all children need to know that someone, somewhere, loves them. I still remember the very first Bible class I attended. It was Easter Sunday, and I guess I was about six, probably Savannah's age."

Titus tried to picture Isabella as a young orphan brought to church by the shelter or foster home where she lived. He imagined her sad eyes, as well as her desire to know that someone cared, and it pierced his heart.

"The teacher had placed a coloring page at everyone's seat. I'll never forget it had a cross in the middle." She smiled. "I colored it purple, but the teacher didn't correct me. She just said that I did a great job coloring. I didn't get a lot of compliments back then, so that one meant a lot."

Again, he imagined Isabella at Savannah's age, sitting in a classroom and happy that the teacher had noticed her paper.

"Then she talked about Jesus dying on a cross, and she said that He did that because He loved us. She sat in front of the class and mentioned each of us by name, you know, like 'Jesus loves Lacy. And Jesus loves Jonathan. And Jesus loves Isabella.'" They'd nearly reached the fountain, and Isabella gazed at the splashing water as she added, "I'll never forget the way my heart felt when she said that, that He loves me."

"I can't imagine what that was like for you." He couldn't remember a time when his parents didn't tell him often that he was loved, not only by them but also by God. "No child should have to wonder whether they're loved."

She continued looking at the fountain, and Titus wondered if it was because she knew she wouldn't be able to hold it together if she looked his way.

"After that Sunday, I knew that even if times seemed tough, He was still there and He loved me. I just had to have faith that He'd see me through."

The intensity of their conversation pressed down on Titus with the weight of a boulder, much more forceful than any emotions he'd shared with anyone else over the past few years. He thought about how mad he was with God. And the fact that he still had a hard time thinking about praying to Someone who'd allowed Savannah to be so hurt. "My faith must not be as strong as yours," he admitted, knowing he wasn't ready to let God back in his life yet.

"If it were just you, it wouldn't be difficult, would it?" she asked. "You're mad at Him because you think He should have spared Savannah from being hurt. But the things I went through in the past have actually made me closer to God now, more dependent on Him. That may be what will happen with Savannah, too. When I had a hard time, I had faith that God would be there."

They'd reached the fountain, and only one of the wrought iron benches surrounding it was vacant, so Titus led her to that bench and sat while he thought about what she'd said. "That's a lot of faith for a kid to have."

"I've always found that children have an easier time with faith than adults. It's simpler for them to believe something they can't see, don't you think?" she asked, as a few geese spotted the brown bag between them and waddled over squawking loudly.

"Yeah, it is." Another ripple of animosity toward God trickled down Titus's spine. He

needed to get his mind off Nan and the un-
ending disappointment, so he opened the bag
and held it toward Isabella. "They're acting
hungry, even if I'm sure they've been eating
all afternoon."

She grabbed a handful of bread and tossed
it toward the geese nearing her feet. Sure
enough, the birds aggressively went after the
tiny pieces as though they hadn't eaten in a
week, while Isabella grinned at their assault.

Titus was thankful for her smile. He needed
it now, needed something to remind him that
life could go on. Plus, that smile reminded
him of Savannah's smile earlier, and the beautiful laugh he'd heard from her at the ice-
cream shop. Everything *could* be okay again.
He just had to keep telling himself that and
believe it. Somehow, as he sat beside Isabella,
he sensed that it might be true.

"I always wondered what this would be
like," she said, while the geese continued
squawking and gobbling the bits of bread.

He was grateful for the change of conversation. "Feeding geese at the town square?"

"No," she said, "being a part of a small
town. Seeing how people live and enjoy them-

selves without all the bright lights and high price tags."

Another glimpse into her past, and Titus tucked it away with the other tidbits he'd learned. "And what do you think?"

"It's as wonderful as I imagined," she said, her voice wistful, depicting the type of longing he'd seen in her eyes when she'd looked at Jacob earlier.

Since her attention was focused on the birds gathering around for the crumbs she tossed their way, Titus took advantage of the opportunity to take in the beauty of the woman who continued to surprise him and touch his heart. Her hair had been damp from the pool when they arrived at the ice-cream shop, but it'd dried into long auburn waves. If she'd had any makeup on before, it was long gone, but that didn't take away from her natural attractiveness. She had a classic, girl-next-door appearance, a combination of pretty and sweet…with an adorable batch of freckles that made her even more endearing. Yet Titus knew that before she came to Claremont, she'd experienced big-city life, those bright lights she'd mentioned earlier.

Without thinking about how his question would sound, he blurted, "Why did you come here?"

Her eyebrows rose, her face filled with surprise, and she looked as though he'd crossed some kind of line. And again, he was reminded that he hadn't had a lot of one-on-one time with a female in way too long.

"Sorry," he said. "Too personal, right?"

But before she could answer, Dee and Emmie Gillespie neared their bench. Mitch and Kate Gillespie's daughters were easy to recognize, with red hair like their father and a surplus of energy that matched the vibrant hue. Titus hadn't noticed Mitch and Kate sitting on a bench on the opposite side of the fountain, but he did now, and he waved at them while he waited to see what the girls wanted.

"Hey, Mr. Titus," Dee said. She was six, the same age as Savannah. They'd had the same kindergarten teacher last year. Emmie was a couple of years younger.

"Hey, Dee, how are you?"

"I'm fine," she said, her mouth sliding to the side as if determining how to ask a difficult question.

He waited, but when she didn't readily start talking, he asked, "Were you looking for Savannah? Because she went to the toy store with Abi Cutter."

"No," Dee said. "We weren't looking for her."

Emmie, seeing her big sister wasn't getting to the point, interrupted. "We wanted to know if you was going to use all of your bread, because we already threw ours and the birds are still hungry. See?" She pointed to the geese that'd backed up toward the fountain but still squawked loudly in their goal to get to the brown bag in spite of the two redheaded obstacles.

Titus saw Mitch shaking his head in disapproval. "Girls, come back over here and leave Mr. Titus alone. You've already used up all of your bread."

"Hey, it's fine. I wasn't sure whether I'd have time to toss the rest anyway, so y'all have at it," Titus said, handing the bag over to a smiling Emmie.

Dee grinned. "Thanks!" Then she and Emmie darted back to the other side of the fountain, the geese following after them and the squawking increasing with every step.

With the noisy birds lured away, Titus and Isabella were relatively alone, the other couples surrounding the fountain either talking among themselves or simply enjoying the picturesque scene. Titus took in the serenity of the moment, the splashing water providing a soothing and relaxing backdrop for the early summer evening.

He knew he'd pressed too hard when he asked why she came to Claremont, so he made a conscious decision to remain silent while they waited on John and Dana to bring Savannah back. He wouldn't ask all of things he wanted to know. He'd simply enjoy the time sitting on the square with the lady who had touched his daughter's heart.

Isabella should've expected Titus to ask why she'd ended up in Claremont. Even so, she hadn't been prepared. So she selected her words carefully. "I came here for one reason," she said, "but I've stayed for several other reasons." She stopped talking when a toddler who'd wandered away from his parents ventured toward their bench. He wore denim overalls over a red T-shirt and looked like a little farmer in the making. His chubby cheeks lifted with his smile.

She held out her hand toward the little guy as he moved closer. Seeing the action as an invitation, he slapped her hand with an open palm, a toddler rendition of a high five. She laughed.

"Micah, come back over here," his father called, and the boy turned and pattered back to his parents, lounging on a patchwork quilt beneath one of the two large oak trees that bracketed the fountain.

Isabella appreciated the little boy buying her some time. "I love being around children," she said, returning a wave from Micah. "I guess I've known that for a while, but I didn't realize how much until I got the chance to volunteer in Atlanta. One of the reasons I want to stay in Claremont is because I'll get to help lots of children at Willow's Haven." Micah blew her an exaggerated kiss. Moved, she returned the sweet gesture and then listened to a robust belly-giggle from the adorable little boy.

Watching the interaction, Titus said, "You do have a way with kids, especially Savannah."

She hoped he'd believe the truth in her

words, because as much as she liked children in general, her feelings for Savannah were different. "Savannah touches my heart. I look at her and her situation and see myself at that age." She motioned toward Micah and his family, now sharing a bowlful of grapes on the blanket. "All children don't have families like that. At Willow's Haven, I'll have a chance to help kids who don't know what it's like to have a parent's love."

"The way you didn't," Titus said.

"Yes." She shifted on the bench so that she faced him. "I know you feel like Savannah has missed out for the past three years. But she's starting to come out of her shell now, and I meant what I said earlier—she's been so very blessed to have you. She *wasn't* all alone. If I'd have had a parent that loved me, even if only one parent, I'd have been so much happier. Savannah may have seemed sad and lost, but even though she was confused about Nan leaving, she knew that you loved her. And that makes all the difference in the world."

He looked as though her words hurt, and Isabella wondered if she'd said something wrong.

"I can't get over the fact that you had no

one in those years growing up," he said, letting her know that his thoughts weren't solely on Savannah, but also on Isabella.

"I had lots of people in my life," she clarified, "but no one who really cared." She thought about some of the worst situations she'd endured. The houses where the lights went out at dark, regardless of the fact that "dark" occurred at 6:00 p.m. The one home where time-out happened in the tiny pantry. She'd been in there for over three hours one night listening to horrid noises from the cupboards. She'd known the house had mice, and she knew where they lingered. In that pantry.

She pushed the chilling memory aside.

"What happened to you after those years were over?" he asked. "I assume you stay in the state's care, whether in an orphanage or foster home, until you're eighteen. But what happens in that system after you become an adult?"

His question tossed Isabella back to her senior year of high school and the doubts and fears that had quadrupled as she prepared for her eighteenth birthday. "It really depends on where you end up," she said.

"Where you end up?"

"Some kids are with families that are willing to see them through college, although that's often only because the state will keep sending them money while the child is enrolled in school. Others get jobs, minimum wage, of course, but they have a way to survive and try to make it on their own. Then some just disappear, turning to easy ways to make money, like stealing or selling drugs. Or selling themselves." She recalled how many of her foster siblings ended up in prison. Or dead. "Things could've turned out differently for me," she said, more to herself than to Titus. "I should be thankful he got me away from the other options."

"Who?" Titus asked. "Your husband?"

She nodded, her thoughts pushing back to when she'd met Richard at the University of Georgia career day. Her high school had taken the seniors on a bus from Atlanta to Athens so they could talk to those who were successful in their choice of study. Isabella had no idea what she would study in college or if she even planned to go to a university. She had the option of moving to a girls' home, basically a place for kids who had aged out of the orphanage but still planned to attend school funded by the state. But when she visited the place, she'd seen no sense of purpose in any of the girls' eyes. They'd all looked so sad. Hopeless.

Isabella had gone to UGA that day thinking that she wasn't willing to pursue college if it meant she'd have to live in that home. But then she'd happened upon the good-looking young real estate magnate already making his mark on the Southeast, even though he was merely twenty-eight. And Richard singled her out immediately, talking to her about life and dreams and goals. He'd asked her out on the spot, and she'd told him she had to wait until she was eighteen, since the orphanage wouldn't allow her to date. That seemed to only intrigue him more, and on her eighteenth birthday, he'd given her roses, an expensive dress, and then taken her to an elaborate restaurant in Atlanta, where he enjoyed teaching her the etiquette of fine dining.

It was *Pretty Woman*, except she wasn't a prostitute—she was an orphan. But Richard Gray might as well have been Richard Gere with all of the attention he poured into Isabella.

"Isabella," Titus said softly, pulling her

from her memories, "can you tell me what happened?"

"Basically, he saved me. He taught me about life. Gave me anything and everything I ever wanted." She thought about how badly she'd wanted children and added, "For the most part."

Titus ran a hand through his hair, and Isabella watched the waves fall into place. "He gave you everything you wanted? Or everything *he* decided you should want?"

Isabella didn't feel right talking badly about everything Richard did for her back then, because without him, she could've ended up in the same type of survival mode as her foster siblings. Living on the streets. Never knowing where she'd get her next meal or where she'd sleep at the end of the day. "He wanted to help me," she said.

Titus started to say something, but then he saw Savannah and Abi skipping across the square toward the fountain. He placed his hand on the bench near hers, then slid his fingers so that they rested on the top of her hand, the warmth of them seeping through like a balm to her soul. "I want to talk to you more about this." He looked at her, and she found herself captivated by the tiny flecks of gold in his earnest hazel eyes.

Before she met Titus, Isabella had only talked to one person about her past. Nan. But she could sense that Titus truly cared. And she wanted to talk to him, spend more time with him, get to know more about this man. "Okay."

"Daddy! Miss Isabella! Look what Mr. John got me!" Savannah clutched a fabric doll with pink yarn hair as she ran ahead of Abi to their bench. "Isn't she cute?"

Abi had a matching doll with turquoise hair. They had button eyes and calico dresses, appearing like something from olden days.

"She *is* cute," Isabella said. "I love her dress, too."

"We won't be able to fix her hair though," Savannah said with a grin. "'Cause it stays this way 'cause it's sewed down."

"You bought her a doll?" Titus asked John.

"He's never been able to tell Abi no," Dana said, nudging his arm with her shoulder. "But he doesn't spoil her too much."

"Daddy says you do," Abi said, "but I don't mind."

John laughed, ran his hand over the top of

her hair. "Yeah, well, Landon is right. And I'm sure you don't mind." Then he tilted his head toward Savannah. "She and Abi had a fit over the new vintage-style dolls Mr. Feazell got in today, and I wanted to get them one. I hope that's okay with you, Titus."

Savannah had been hugging her doll, but she stopped and looked at her daddy. "It is, isn't it, Daddy? Because this is the best day ever. I went swimming and we had ice cream and then I got a new doll."

Isabella watched emotions play over his face. Savannah had made so much progress today at the pool and now again with her disposition, practically beaming as she stood beside her friend holding her new doll.

"Yes, it's fine," he said. "But what do you tell Mr. John and Miss Dana?"

She turned to face John and Dana. "Thank you so much!"

"You're welcome," they said, as Jacob started rubbing his eyes and whimpering.

"It's about bedtime for little man," Dana said. "It was good to run into y'all here. I guess we'll see you at the pool again tomorrow?"

"Definitely," Titus said. He turned to Isabella. "As long as that works for you?"

They hadn't missed a day since they'd started, and she certainly wouldn't miss one now that Savannah had finally made her way into the water. "Definitely."

Chapter Eight

I wanted to be a good mom.

Titus sipped his first cup of coffee Sunday morning and reflected on how differently the weekend had turned out than he had planned. Friday afternoon had gone amazingly well, with Isabella getting Savannah to put her face beneath the water at the end of her swim lesson. Titus had watched in awe as Isabella slowly and gently continued to draw his little girl out of her shell, and his admiration increased each time they were together.

In fact, he'd asked her if she wanted to take another trip to the square with them after the lesson ended, but she'd made plans with Savvy to drive to a furniture store in Stockville to start shopping for the future cabins at Willow's Haven. Titus would be lying if he said he wasn't disappointed that he hadn't been able to spend more time with her on Friday evening, but he'd resolved that he and Savannah would go to the B and B on Saturday and see if she wanted to do something outdoors with them. Maybe go on a picnic at Hydrangea Park, hike to Jasper Falls or go horseback riding at the Cutter Dude Ranch. Anything that would let him spend more time with Isabella and have a chance to pick up their conversation where they'd left off Thursday night.

But then he and Savannah had arrived home Friday evening to find the brown box waiting on his porch. All desire to have a good time this weekend dissipated. He'd moved the thing inside, and it still sat where he'd placed it on the table in the foyer. Thankfully, Savannah had been so excited about her progress at the pool and eager to play with the new doll John Cutter had bought her that she'd barely noticed the package.

Titus, on the other hand, couldn't stop staring at the brown square—larger than a shoebox but smaller than he'd expected for a container that supposedly held everything someone had left behind.

Everything that Nan had left behind.

Yesterday, instead of getting in touch with Isabella and seeing if she wanted to spend time at the park, the square or the dude ranch, he and Savannah had stayed home. She'd played with her dolls and spent a little time on the swing set in the backyard, while Titus managed to smile and interact with her as though everything was normal. As though he weren't fighting an inner battle deciding whether to open that box.

Now, though he drank his coffee on the front porch, he still felt the tension of knowing that his wife's belongings were fewer than ten feet away. He wanted to know what was inside. And he didn't want to know. What if she'd left something that told him exactly why she abandoned them three years ago and that knowledge finally did his heart in?

What good would it do to know now?

The screen door squeaked as it opened, and Savannah stepped outside. She wore her favorite pink nightgown, the one with Strawberry Shortcake on the front. It was probably too short now, the ruffled edge that used to hit her ankles barely passing her knees, but she loved it, and Titus wouldn't take away anything she loved. Ever.

"Daddy?"

He sat in one of the wooden rockers, and he motioned for her to join him the way she often did on weekend mornings when he didn't have to work. Titus had awakened before six and come to the porch to watch the sunrise, his typical beginning to a Sunday morning. Before Nan left, they began their week together enjoying the Sunday-morning sunrise, often combined with a short devotional and prayer.

Titus had wanted to see the sunrise this morning, but he wasn't in the mood to pray, especially not today, with that box sitting just a few feet inside the door. He mustered up a smile for his princess. "Hey, sweetie. Did you sleep well?" He placed his coffee mug on the table nearby and opened his arms so she could climb onto his lap.

"Yes, sir," she said, her voice still wobbly from sleep. She squirmed into his arms and nestled her head beneath his chin as she curled into her usual position, her knees pulling against the fabric of her gown. Her hair was soft against his face and smelled of the no-tears shampoo she'd picked out the last time they went to the store. It wasn't as tangled as usual, suggesting she did sleep well, and Titus was glad for that.

He slowly rocked, knowing she'd need her normal amount of time to wake. Like her mom, Savannah wasn't a morning person, at least not at first. She'd take her time waking up, drift back to sleep a couple of times before deciding that she was ready to begin the day and then find that burst of energy to see her through to the evening. Right now in his arms, her breathing had grown heavy, and Titus knew without looking that her eyes were closed, her doll held tight, and she was catching another little nap before deciding to start her day.

Savannah had always been a snuggler— that was the term Nan had used—and Titus wasn't sure if he'd ever appreciated the tender quality more than now. He needed to hold the one constant in his life, the little girl who meant so much to him that it ripped him apart to see her hurt. Right now, though, she didn't seem to be hurting. In fact, over the past week, she'd begun a transformation from the timid, sad child whose mom left three years ago to a happy, smiling little girl who looked forward to every day, swim lessons and new friends and dolls. And Miss Isabella.

Titus had the sudden impulse to say a prayer of thanks to God, but he pushed the urge away. He still wasn't certain why God had allowed all of this to happen to his precious child, and he wasn't prepared to talk to Him without that frustration pressing through every word.

After rocking a few moments, she stirred in his arms and raised her head. "Daddy, can we have pancakes?"

He kissed her forehead. "Sure."

"With bananas on top?"

"I think I can arrange that," he said, truly enjoying their time together. "You want me to make them now, or you want to wait awhile?"

"Let's wait awhile," she said, sleepily laying her head on his chest.

Titus patted her back as he started rocking again. "That sounds like a good plan." He watched the sun begin a steady ascent above Lookout Mountain and expected her to drift back off, but then she popped her head up, hazel eyes blinking into alertness.

"Daddy, is today Sunday?"

Knowing the probable reason for her question, Titus felt a hint of dread as he answered. "Yes, today's Sunday."

"So we need to get ready for church, right? Can I wear my blue dress?"

He'd bought her the sundress and a few other new clothing items on the day he'd gotten the contract for Willow's Haven, but she hadn't had a chance to wear it yet. She'd asked the same question last Sunday, when she'd wanted to go to church, and Titus had told her they weren't going, that he needed to stay home. He'd then offered to take her outside to play, and that had satisfied her for the day.

Today, however, with the look of hope in her eyes, he didn't know how he'd turn her down. And he didn't know how he'd go back to church when he wasn't on good terms with God.

Her eyebrows dipped, and her lower lip eased out. "Do you have to stay home again?"

Titus hated disappointing her, but as he thought about that brown box and everything else God had dealt him over the past three years, he simply couldn't forget and pretend to worship Him today. "Yeah, sweetie, I do."

Her head dropped back to his chest, and she clutched her doll tighter.

Titus took a deep breath. He couldn't bear making her sad. He'd simply have to suck it up and—

"Daddy?" She lifted her head and looked at him with her eyes wide.

"Yes?"

"I could go with Rose and Daisy." Her hopeful tone couldn't be ignored, and Titus was extremely grateful that she'd thought of a way to allow her to be happy and keep him from feeling hypocritical by entering the church doors and merely going through the motions of worshipping.

"That's a good idea," he said. "I'll call Miss Savvy and get started making your pancakes. You can go put on your blue dress."

"Can Miss Isabella fix my hair? I want it pretty when I wear my new dress."

Savannah had grown so accustomed to having Isabella style her hair each morning during the week that Titus wasn't surprised she thought of her now. And he actually had Isabella's number, since she'd given it to him

Friday in case they wanted to practice swimming on Saturday.

He knew he could call Isabella this morning and she'd probably offer to come over and fix Savannah's hair in a style she'd love, but that would also give her the opportunity to convince him to go to church. And Titus was certain he didn't want to go. He was also certain that, after receiving Nan's box, he didn't need to do anything that might tempt him to jump into a relationship with anyone. Even Isabella. "I can fix your hair this morning," he said. When she looked doubtful, he added, "And if you want it done differently, I'm sure Miss Savvy can help when they come to pick you up."

"Okay," she said, her voice somber.

"And don't forget to model the dress for me, and make sure you wear those new shoes we bought."

The request received the desired reaction. She smiled. "I will." Then she wrapped her arms around his neck and squeezed. "Love you, Daddy."

"I love you, too," he said, glad that she wanted to go to church. In spite of his own misgivings toward God, he was thankful that she hadn't given up on Him, too.

"Isabella, I'm so glad you came to lunch with us," Savvy said, as the twins and Savannah dashed to the dessert bar for a post-meal treat.

"I appreciate you inviting me." She'd been glad for the chance to go out with the large group from church, many of whom were quickly becoming more than mere acquaintances. People she could classify as friends. Dana and John Cutter, with baby Jacob between them; Brodie, Savvy, Dylan and the twins; Daniel Brantley, the youth minister, his wife, Mandy, and their children, Kaden and Mia; and David and Laura Presley with their babies, Grace and Joy. The group had pushed a bunch of tables together so that they filled an entire side of the buffet restaurant in Stockville that specialized in Southern home-style cooking.

Isabella listened to the laughter, the chatting children and the discussion about Brother Henry's lesson with something close to awe. *This* was what small-town living was all about—families, friendships, people sharing a meal and sharing love. Her happiness at being included caused her chest to tighten, and she mentally attempted to control the burst of emotion overwhelming her soul.

"Hey, you okay?" Savvy sat to Isabella's right, and she'd apparently noticed her palpable reaction to her surroundings.

Isabella forced a smile. "Just very happy to be here with all of you," she said. "I don't merely mean at the restaurant—" She couldn't complete the sentence.

"I know exactly what you mean," Savvy said, offering an understanding smile. "Hard to believe I ran away from all of this, from life in Claremont, when I was eighteen, but thankfully, with a little help from my friend Willow and from God, I found my way back." She smiled as Rose, Daisy and Savannah returned to the table, their plates filled with brownies and strawberries. "I can't imagine anywhere I'd rather be."

"Me, either," Isabella said. "But..." Her attention moved to Savannah, biting into a fat strawberry. She'd seemed happy at church this morning, but Isabella was certain that she'd have been even happier if Titus had been there, too.

"He'll come around," Savvy said, knowing where Isabella's thoughts had headed. "He's gone through more pain in the past few years than some people experience in a lifetime. I can see why he's not so happy with God right now, but Titus has always had a strong faith. That'll come back, I'm sure." She looked toward the girls, probably to make sure they weren't listening. "When we picked up Savannah this morning, I told him that we were praying for him and that we'd keep praying."

Isabella nodded. "I've been praying for him, too."

"Then I have no doubt that everything will work out," Savvy said.

Isabella said a prayer that Savvy was right.

"Miss Isabella?"

She turned toward Savannah, watching her from the opposite end of the table. "Yes, Savannah?"

"You didn't get dessert." She had a brownie in her hand as she made the statement, and she held it toward Isabella. "You want some of mine? I've got strawberries, too, if you like them better than brownies."

Savvy whispered, "Precious," and Isabella agreed. Savannah's sweet spirit and giving nature touched her heart. In spite of everything she'd been through, she wanted to help others, even if that meant giving up her own dessert. "I'll get something," she said, "but thank you for offering to share."

"You're welcome," she said, smiling before taking a bite of the brownie in her hand.

"She cares about you," Savvy whispered.

"I know," Isabella quietly returned. "I care about her, too." Knowing Savannah was watching her to see if she'd follow through on getting her dessert, she scooted her chair back from the table and headed to the dessert bar. She didn't want to disappoint Savannah. And she'd told Savvy the truth; she honestly cared about Savannah more than she'd have thought possible a few weeks ago. However, Savannah wasn't the only member of the Jameson family that had captured Isabella's thoughts and pulled at her heart.

She should be happy that Titus had decided to keep his distance. But in spite of her misgivings toward men in general and the fact that she shouldn't want to get all that close to one after her past with Richard, she hadn't realized how much she looked forward to seeing Titus each morning at Willow's Haven and each afternoon at the pool until it didn't happen. Yesterday, she'd expected him to call or maybe even show up at the B and B, because she'd hoped he might have missed her the way she'd missed him. When he hadn't, she'd thought she'd possibly still see him at church this morning. But that hadn't happened, either.

She got a small bowl of peach cobbler topped with a scoop of ice cream and went back to the table to join in the conversation and attempt to get her thoughts off the handsome construction worker. But he'd remained on her mind since she first got to town, and a bowl of cobbler and ice cream didn't change that. In fact, as the group discussed upcoming plans for the Fourth of July weekend, Isabella's thoughts wandered to the most vivid memories of the past two weeks.

Titus, riding the bulldozer across the property at Willow's Haven that first late afternoon. Titus, watching Isabella braid Savannah's hair and telling his little girl that she was beautiful. Titus, clenching his jaw and blinking past tears as he listened to Savannah tell Isabella she loved her. Titus, listening to

Isabella talk about her past and looking at her with eyes that said he understood and cared.

"Isabella, is that okay with you?" Savvy asked.

She wasn't certain how long she'd zoned out while she'd been consumed in thoughts of Titus Jameson. "I'm sorry, what?"

Savvy grinned, leaned close to Isabella. "Dare I guess who you're thinking about?" While Isabella's cheeks burned, Savvy laughed. "You don't have to answer, and I'm pretty sure I'm the only one that noticed you were distracted."

Isabella sighed. "I'm glad for that." Then she remembered that Savvy had asked her a question. "You asked if something was okay with me?"

"Yes," Savvy said. "Stockville College, where Brodie coaches baseball, is nearby, and he wants to check on the field house since we're here, so I was wondering if you wouldn't mind taking Savannah home. Titus lives on Main Street, only four blocks from the B and B."

Isabella glanced at the other people at the table and was certain each of them knew exactly where Titus lived. She, on the other hand, was probably one of the few people in town who didn't. She also suspected that Brodie didn't have to go to the field house now and that this request was more than likely a not-too-discreet setup. She wasn't so sure how Titus would feel about her showing up at his home. If he'd wanted to see her, he'd have called yesterday. "Savvy, I don't think…"

Savvy placed her palm on Isabella's shoulder. "I know you think I'm asking for you," she said. "But trust me, I'm asking just as much for Titus. He's been alone for too long, and anyone would have to be crazy not to notice how you two look at each other." She lifted a shoulder. "Besides, I'm just asking you to give Savannah a ride home. Whether he asks you to stay and visit, or whatever, is totally up to him. And whether you decide to stop pretending that you aren't crazily attracted to our construction guy is totally up to you."

Isabella didn't know what to say. Yes, she was attracted to Titus. But that didn't mean she wanted a relationship with the guy. She did, however, really want to see him.

Savvy didn't wait for her to respond. She

turned toward the girls and asked, "Savannah, would you like to ride with Miss Isabella? We've got to go to Mr. Brodie's work for a little while, but she can take you home. Okay?"

Savannah practically glowed, her smile claiming her face. "Yes!"

Isabella couldn't argue now if she tried, and Savvy knew it. "You're sneaky," she said.

Brodie had been paying his bill, but he walked over and held out a to-go sack for Isabella. "This is for Titus. I figure you can take it to him, right?"

"How do you know he hasn't already eaten?" Isabella asked.

"He's a guy, and he's got nobody to feed but himself today," he said. "Trust me, he hasn't eaten."

Bewildered by the blatant conspiring of the couple, she accepted the bag. "You're in on this, too?" she asked Brodie.

He shrugged, while Savvy giggled. "Don't worry," she said. "You can thank us later."

Chapter Nine

If I'd have known then what I know now...

There was something about the scent of sawdust that invigorated Titus, gave him a sense of accomplishment and pushed aside every ounce of tension. He'd loved the smell ever since he was a boy, when he and his father spent hours cutting and designing Titus's car each year for the local pinewood derby. It hadn't taken him long to realize how much he enjoyed building, creating something functional from little more than wood and nails. No matter how stressed he felt, he could count on his love of constructing to clear his mind, give him peace.

Today was no different. He'd wanted to

replace the old porch rails, rotted from water damage, for at least a year but hadn't made the time. However, as soon as Brodie and Savvy had picked up Savannah, he'd hauled his table saw to the front yard, set up the miter saw on the tailgate of his truck and started a project that, if he worked every spare minute, should be done before the day ended. That should be plenty of time for his place to match the other Main Street homes for next weekend's Fourth of July activities.

It'd taken him hardly any time at all to rip out the weathered rails, and Titus wondered why he'd waited so long to start the repairs. The things were an eyesore, and he already felt better, even though the missing rails currently made the front porch look like a mouth with more than its share of lost teeth.

He wiped the sweat from his brow and took another look at the front of the house. Now that he allowed himself to really examine it, he noticed that much more than the porch rails needed repair. He spotted a couple of shingles curled up at the edges, and the trim desperately needed a fresh coat of paint. Trying to remember the last time he'd put any elbow grease into his own home, he was surprised to realize that it'd been before Nan's departure.

The symbolism of him being so eager to fix the place up this morning wasn't lost on him. For the past three years, he'd been stuck in the past, hanging on to what used to be and shirking even the mere thought of moving forward, of starting anything new, when it came to something that he'd shared with Nan. But that life had truly ended now, the box that sat in his foyer a potent reminder of the fact, and Titus needed to accept that reality and move on. Not only for his sake, but for his daughter's.

Ready to cut another set of railings, he grabbed the pencil from behind his ear, measured off the two-by-four and brought it to the table saw. Focused on the task at hand, he didn't notice the car pull into the driveway. However, after the final cut, he turned…and his breath caught in his throat.

Dazzling. The word slammed his thoughts and stayed there, an accurate depiction of the vision that had exited the car and stood watching him work.

Isabella's hair cascaded in a waterfall of red-brown waves falling past her shoulders.

She wore a bright yellow dress that tapered in at the center, drawing attention to her waist and accenting her petite features. Red heels peeked out beneath the long hem, and she wore matching red jewelry. The red lipstick, however, carried Titus's gaze to her mouth and made him wonder...

"Hey, Daddy!" Savannah climbed from the back of Isabella's car, her fabric doll in one hand and some type of Popsicle stick and crepe paper collection in the other. "We learned about Peter, James and John in the sailboat. See?" She held up the craft and, after dragging his eyes away from Isabella, Titus perceived the image of a sailboat.

"Beautiful," he said, referring not only to his daughter's creation but also to the woman now crossing the lawn, her red heels dipping into the soft grass with every step and reminding him of one of those crazy romance movies where the couple crosses a field in a hazy sun-drenched effect, looking far too perfect and far too rehearsed.

Nothing about Isabella walking toward him looked rehearsed. Her mouth quivered a bit, as though she wasn't quite sure what to say, and she teetered once when her heel sank a little too deep into the ground.

"Brodie and Savvy needed to go to the college after lunch, so they asked if I could bring Savannah home." She raised her right hand, and Titus noticed a bag that appeared to hold a to-go box. He wasn't surprised that he hadn't noticed the bag before—he'd been too smitten by the woman carrying it. "Have you eaten?"

Titus's stomach growled at the mere thought of food, and he grinned. "Kind of forgot about eating."

"We had a big lunch," Savannah said. "I ate potatoes and green beans and meat, and then I got strawberries and brownies for dessert."

Titus's interest in the to-go bag increased. "I'm guessing y'all went to the buffet in Stockville?"

"We did," Isabella said. "And I have to admit I've never had that much of a selection of home-style cooking in one place."

He laughed. "Yeah, it's a favorite around here for Sunday lunch, or any other meal, for that matter. Three sisters own it, and they use the recipes that've been handed down in their family for generations."

"You can thank Brodie for this," she said. "I'd have gotten you a plate, but I honestly didn't think of it, and I didn't know I'd be coming here after lunch."

He couldn't read her face to know whether that had been an inconvenience. "I appreciate you giving Savannah a ride home and bringing the food."

"Oh, it wasn't any trouble at all." She extended the bag. "I guess you'll probably want to get started on your lunch." She seemed hesitant, as though uncertain whether he wanted her here. And she also seemed ready to leave as soon as she handed over the food.

It made him a little less eager to take it.

"Miss Isabella, can you stay? You could see all of my dolls and I could show you my swing set." Savannah's hopeful tone said Titus wasn't the only one who didn't want Isabella to go.

"I, um…" Isabella glanced at Titus. "I don't want to intrude."

He hadn't missed her uncertainty at being here, so he wanted to make sure she understood. "You're not intruding," he said. "And Savannah would love for you to stay and visit, if you don't have other plans."

"I don't," she said.

"I'm going to put on my play clothes, and I'll be right back!" Savannah hurried inside, the screen door slamming behind her.

Isabella continued holding the bag toward Titus, and he now accepted it, their fingers touching with the exchange.

"Wanna walk inside with me while I get a glass of tea to go with this?" he asked. "Are you thirsty? I'll fix you one, too."

"Sure," she said, lifting the hem of her dress to more easily make her way up the steps.

"Hang on, let me get these out of the way." He kicked a couple of wood scraps to clear the path across the porch.

"Thanks."

He noticed she'd spoken no more than necessary and that she still had a look of hesitation, and he thought he knew why. He didn't want her doubting whether he wanted her here. "Just in case you're wondering," he said, feeling a sense of rightness at letting her know, "Savannah isn't the only one who wants you to stay."

She blinked, her cheeks turning pink as she stopped just shy of the door. "I—thought I'd hear from you yesterday," she said, and then looked away, as though she hadn't intended to say so much. But the fact that she'd *wanted* to hear from him meant a lot and, truthfully, he'd missed seeing her as well, had thought about her ever since they'd parted Friday afternoon.

If he hadn't found that package on his porch Friday night, he'd have called her, spent time with her, enjoyed the beautiful weekend instead of being consumed by the past. "It was a rough day," he admitted. "I'll tell you about it, but I don't want to chance Savannah hearing the conversation." He opened the door so she could enter. "Can you stay awhile? Maybe we'll get a chance to talk about it later."

Isabella couldn't imagine anything she'd rather do than stay. She'd been nervous showing up without an invitation, in spite of the fact that she'd brought Savannah home. Richard had abhorred anyone arriving at their home without an appointment or invitation. But Titus, in his navy T-shirt and well-worn jeans, both sprinkled with the sawdust that emphasized his hardworking status, looked as though he'd be disappointed if she didn't say yes, even though he was clearly busy.

She didn't want to leave. "Yes, I can stay."

His smile, reaching his eyes, said she hadn't misjudged the invitation. He wasn't merely being hospitable. He wanted her here, with him and with Savannah. Joy whispered through her at the realization. Then she stepped inside and saw the box on the foyer table, the return address of the charity hospital written in dark, bold print at the top left corner. She knew from their previous conversation that a box of Nan's things was coming, and she could see now that it had arrived... and was still unopened.

Titus followed her gaze and heaved a sigh. "Like I said, rough day." Then he stepped between her and the box, waiting until her attention returned to his face. His eyes drew her in, and she felt her pulse increase as she stood so near to him, her concern for what he'd felt when he received that package washing over her, as well as the desire to say something, do something, to help this man.

"I don't want to talk about it now," he said quietly, as Savannah's footsteps could be heard from upstairs. "Right now, I want to get a couple of glasses of tea, take them out on the porch and visit with you while I eat this delicious lunch you brought." He smiled. "Sound good?"

"Yes," she said. "Sounds good." She followed him through the house, decorated in antique furnishings and vintage fabrics of slate blue and golden yellow that embodied warmth and contentment. She loved the style, the feel, of the home and thought it suited the man who lived here.

While Titus fixed the iced tea, she took the opportunity to continue examining the house. She'd already been captivated by the outside, with the wraparound porch and antebellum style she'd always admired, but the inside was equally compelling. The ceilings were high, at least twelve feet, and the architecture something that even Richard would have respected. Stained glass accented each window, as well as the kitchen light fixtures that hovered overhead like illuminated floral arrangements on display. The boldly carved crown molding beautifully accented the dark cabinetry, desks and bookshelves impeccably positioned throughout the living area and kitchen. "Your home is beautiful."

"Thanks," he said, handing her a glass of iced tea. He picked up the to-go box, some utensils and his own glass, then led the way out of the kitchen. "It was my great-grandparents' home, and then my folks moved in and raised me here. When Nan and I married, they wanted us to have it." They reached the front door and he turned his back to the screen to hold it open while she passed through. "They were looking for a reason to move to the beach. My dad got a job offer he wanted to take, and everything worked out with the timing of our wedding and the job offer for them to go."

"What does your dad do?" she asked, following him to the front porch swing.

"He's a real estate agent." He laughed. "Never had a whole lot of business around here because people pretty much find a place they like and keep it, or pass it down to the next generation, like this place." He set his tea on a table nearby and opened the to-go box. "I *thought* this smelled like chicken and dressing," he said appreciatively.

Isabella surveyed the contents—chicken and dressing, cranberry sauce, green beans, coleslaw and a roll. "Oh, Brodie didn't put anything in for dessert. I should've looked in the box, and I'd have gotten you something. The dessert bar was amazing."

"I've seen it before." He winked. "No worries. I'm not big on sweets, anyway."

She recalled the way he'd eaten that ice cream Thursday evening. "You sure seemed to like ice cream."

He'd already taken a couple of big bites of dressing and cranberry sauce, but he stopped eating and held his fork in the air. "Yeah, well, that had more to do with the company and the occasion than with the dessert." He took another bite. "We had to celebrate Savannah's success in the pool, and she loves ice cream." Another bite, and then he looked at her thoughtfully. "You've done so much for Savannah since you came to town," he said. "I hope you know how much that means to me."

As if on cue, Savannah pushed through the screen door. She'd changed into a pink T-shirt and denim shorts, and her feet were bare.

Titus noticed. "Savannah, I'm working with nails today. I'm not so sure it's smart for you to be out here without shoes."

She frowned. "But I don't like to wear them."

He took a bite of green beans, a sip of tea, and then continued. "I know you don't like them, but you need them, at least until I finish working and get everything cleaned up."

Her shoulders lifted and fell with her dramatic sigh. "Is that going to take too long?"

"Probably the rest of today, but I'm hoping to be done before tomorrow," he said. "So go put on your tennis shoes, please."

"Yes, sir." She turned and headed inside, her footsteps on the stairs echoing as she hurried back to her room in search of shoes.

Isabella sipped her tea, the cool liquid deliciously sweet and refreshing. A breeze wafted through the porch, and she thought of how perfect this felt, sitting on a porch swing with Titus and waiting for Savannah to return. She obviously hadn't been happy about his directive to don shoes, but she'd obeyed him without complaint. Impressed with how tenderly yet fatherly he treated his little girl, she said, "You're so good with her."

"It isn't that difficult," he said. "As long as she understands that my corrections are done with love, she doesn't mind them."

"I always wondered what it'd be like, having a child."

He'd been gently easing the swing back and forth with his feet as he ate and while they chatted, but he planted his soles and slowed the swing to a stop. "Did y'all try to have children? Or think about adopting?" he asked. "I'll admit that I wondered, but I didn't think I should ask. But since you mentioned it..."

Like many of the other topics she'd broached with Titus, this one had only been shared with one person. Nan. But Isabella did want to talk about it, and she couldn't think of anyone who'd listen better than the man beside her on the swing. "I wanted a baby immediately, as soon as Richard and I married," she admitted.

When she didn't readily continue, he prodded, "But..."

"But Richard said he wanted me to get my education, so I did. I got the degree in business administration." She decided not to tell Titus that Richard refused to let her use the degree to get a job.

"Okay, so that took four years. But you said y'all were together for ten. What happened after that?" he asked.

"After that, when I continued to ask about having a baby, he finally told me the truth.

He said that he didn't think I had the kind of background a woman needed to raise a child, since I never had a real mother and the women that had me in their homes weren't anything like the type of mother figure he'd want raising his children. And he wouldn't consider adoption, because he said that you didn't know the physical or emotional genetic history of the child," she said, remembering how terribly those words had stung. Growing up, she'd been one of those children praying to be adopted. "Those were a couple of the reasons, but the main reason…" She knew Titus wouldn't like this.

"Go on."

"Richard didn't like the way women looked after childbirth. He said their bodies were never the same, and he didn't want that for his wife." Isabella almost didn't add the rest, but she decided if she were telling Titus some of it, she might as well tell it all. "I told him I'd heard of some surgeons who could make certain I looked the same after the baby was born." Tears threatened as she recalled begging her husband to let her have a child. She swallowed. "He said it wouldn't matter. I wouldn't be the same. Then he said that he should be enough for me, that I didn't need anyone else to love."

Titus closed the lid on the box, even though he hadn't finished his food, and placed it on the table beside his tea. "Your husband was a first-class idiot."

Isabella didn't know what she'd expected him to say, but that wasn't it, and his bluntness caught her so off guard that she found herself laughing. Hard. "Titus, you—" she giggled "—you really shouldn't say that."

"Just speaking the truth," he said, but the grin that now played with his mouth said he didn't mind making her laugh.

Isabella didn't mind it, either.

Savannah scurried onto the porch as if she thought she'd missed something. "What're you laughing at?" she asked, but apparently just the sound of them laughing caused her to giggle, too, which made Isabella laugh even harder.

"Your daddy," Isabella said, pointing to Titus while Savannah hurried to the swing and jumped into his lap.

"Are you being funny, Daddy?" she asked.

He kissed her cheek. "I guess I am."

She smiled, as though that was perfectly

fine in her book. Then she tilted her head and looked at Isabella. "Do you want to go see my dolls now? And maybe my swing set or my playhouse?"

Isabella placed a hand on her stomach as her laughter subsided. "I sure do."

Savannah leaned away from Titus, scanned Isabella's dress and frowned. "But you have on church clothes. How're you going to play?"

Isabella brushed her hand down her skirt. The fabric looked dressy but was actually a cool cotton and very comfortable. "Don't worry. I can play in this."

"What about your shoes?" Savannah shook her head at the strappy red heels. They were higher than any other shoes Isabella owned, but they'd looked so pretty with the dress that she hadn't been able to resist putting them on this morning.

She lifted a foot. "You're right, I probably can't play too well in these, but it's okay. I'll just slip them off."

Savannah's eyebrows shot up, and she turned toward Titus. "Daddy, can Miss Isabella take her shoes off?" she asked, completely serious. And absolutely adorable.

Isabella smiled as she awaited his answer.

He peeked at the offensive shoes. "I'm sure Miss Isabella will be careful where she steps."

"I'd have been careful," Savannah countered.

Titus squeezed her as he added, "*And* Miss Isabella is an adult, so I won't tell her what she can and can't do. You, however, are my daughter, so that happens to be part of my job."

"I'll be very careful," Isabella promised Savannah, and she received the little girl's nod of approval.

"All right then," Savannah said, wiggling out of Titus's embrace, "let me show you the dolls in my room first." She hurried across the porch and opened the screen door.

"Okay," Isabella said, but before she left the swing, she touched Titus's hand. "Thank you."

"For what?"

"For making me laugh," she said. "And for not telling me what I can and can't do."

Chapter Ten

My heart has never been so torn.

As was often the case when Titus was engrossed in his work, the time passed at lightning speed and, before he'd taken another break, the sun started dipping toward the mountains. The primary difference with today's workday and his usual workdays, however, was the woman who occasionally walked out to check on him, bring him a tall glass of iced water or sweet tea and offer an appreciative smile for his progress. Add the fact that his little girl joined Isabella for each visit, and Titus couldn't remember the last time he'd had a better day.

Or worked so hard.

The rotted railings had all been replaced

and primed. He hadn't painted them yet, but he could knock that out tomorrow evening, after Savannah's swim lesson. She must've reminded him six times that he'd promised she could start back at her lessons on Monday. It made him feel guilty that he hadn't called Isabella yesterday and asked her to meet them at the pool for a weekend lesson, but yesterday, as he'd told Isabella before, had been rough.

Today, on the other hand, had been nothing short of amazing.

He swept the last of the sawdust off the porch and began putting away the excess wood and power tools, all the while glancing toward the house and speculating over what the two females were doing inside. He imagined them in Savannah's room, either having a tea party with her dolls or playing a game of Candy Land or pretending to cook at her toy kitchen. Smiling at what he expected to find inside, he finished cleaning up and then headed through the back door.

The delicious smells filling the house told him they hadn't been pretending to cook. They'd been all-out cooking. Entering the kitchen, he had to stop and admire the picturesque scene. Isabella, still wearing the bright yellow dress, faced the opposite direction so she couldn't see his grin as he watched her help Savannah pour chocolate chips into a glass measuring cup. Her feet were still bare, which only added to the beauty of seeing her making herself at home in his kitchen.

Savannah's hair looked wet but had been braided, and she wore her nightgown. She stood on the small stool she typically used to reach the sink in the bathroom. He'd purchased it to help her brush her teeth. Obviously, it was also the right size to reach the kitchen countertop for a cooking lesson.

"Can I taste it yet?" she asked.

Isabella touched Savannah's nose. "Let's wait until we've made the batter into cookies."

"Daddy doesn't let me have dessert until after dinner either," Savannah said glumly. "But how about one chocolate chip?"

"I don't see how one chocolate chip will hurt, or maybe three." Isabella laughed as she placed the tiny chips in Savannah's palm.

Savannah giggled and popped them in her mouth.

Isabella turned her attention back to the

batter in the bowl. "And then we'll spoon this on the cookie sheet, put it in the oven…"

"And go tell Daddy we made dinner!" Savannah cheered.

"Actually, he might already know," Titus said, watching them turn around and then noticing that Isabella wasn't as stain-free as she appeared from the back. The front of her dress had a nice dusting of flour that made this scene look even more real. Even more perfect.

"Daddy!" Savannah jumped off the stool and crossed the kitchen to leap into his arms. "What do you think? Miss Isabella said you'd like it if we made you a bunch of food after you worked all day. Do you like it? Guess what all we made!" She put her hands on each side of his face and placed her face directly in front of his. "Don't look at the table."

Titus purposefully turned his back to the table, where he'd already noticed several dishes in the center, and inhaled appreciatively. "Mmm, roast?"

Savannah bobbed her head while Isabella, smiling, spooned cookie batter onto the sheet. "And what else?" Savannah asked.

He took another whiff. "I'm guessing potatoes, and maybe some carrots?"

"You're a good guesser," she said. "And one more thing. It's something that I don't like."

Isabella's soft laugh trickled across the kitchen as she placed the last dollop of batter on the sheet and then slid it into the oven. "I thought you said you'd never tried it," she reminded Savannah.

"I haven't, but I know I'm not going to like it," Savannah said.

Titus kissed her cheek. She was so adorable, and so undeniably happy. It'd been way too long. "Okay, I give up. What's the thing that you think you don't like?"

"Gravy," Savannah said, crinkling her nose and turning her face to the side as though even the word made her cringe.

He loved homemade gravy. "Really? You made gravy?" His question was directed to Isabella, but Savannah answered.

"Yes, sir. And it took forever! I had to stir and stir and stir." She lifted her right arm. "My hand is wore out."

This time, Isabella's laugh wasn't so soft,

and neither was Titus's. "Well, I sure do appreciate you working so hard for me," he said.

"You're welcome," Savannah answered. "It's 'cause I love you."

His heart swelled. "I love you, too."

"Guess what," she said. "I already took my bath and washed my hair. And Miss Isabella did it so I can sleep with it like this—" she held up the braid "—and then in the morning, even you can fix it."

Isabella had started setting the table, and she glanced up with a smile. "I don't believe I said it quite like that. I said that it'd be something that you could do on the days when you aren't going to see me the next morning."

The comment reminded Titus that he didn't like the mornings when he didn't see her, and it also reminded him that he shouldn't let himself get too used to this, having her around and filling the void that his mother had mentioned. He couldn't deny Isabella had been good for Savannah and had helped her more already than the child psychologists had done in three years. But he also couldn't deny that he wasn't ready to jump into another relationship headfirst after his marriage had ended so badly.

A fact underscored by the box still sitting in his foyer.

He swallowed, determined to enjoy his daughter's happiness and the fact that she and Isabella had spent their afternoon preparing this meal. So he touched Savannah's braid and asked, "How do I fix it?"

"Tell him, Miss Isabella."

Isabella continued putting the utensils on napkins beside the plates as she explained. "You braid her hair after it's washed and towel dried, and leave it that way while she sleeps."

"See, Daddy—easy, huh?"

"Seems that way," he agreed. "And then in the morning?"

"Just undo the braid and finger comb it." Isabella had finished at the table and started getting glasses from the cabinet. "You want sweet tea?"

"I do," he said.

She poured two glasses of tea and placed them beside the plates. Savannah's cup of milk already sat in front of her favorite purple plate, also at the table. "I think we're ready to eat."

"Yum," Savannah said, releasing her hold

on Titus and squirming out of his embrace to reach the floor and then get to the table. "Isn't this great, Daddy?"

"Yes," he said, "it is." And he made a mental note not to get too used to it. Isabella had brought Savannah home and then stayed to help watch after her so he could work, something that probably most of his friends in Claremont would've done. He didn't need to think anything more of it than that, and he shouldn't feel guilty about enjoying this time with her so soon after Nan's death. She was a friend, helping them out by cooking a meal. That was it.

Isabella motioned toward the three place settings. "I kind of invited myself to have dinner with y'all," she said. "Is that okay?"

He pushed Savannah's chair in so she could reach the table better and then took a step toward Isabella. Titus assumed his emotions had been obvious, if she'd have even considered that he might not want her to stay. After everything she'd done for him, everything she'd done for Savannah, he wouldn't ask her to leave. Plus, he wasn't ready for her to go. "More than okay," he said. "And thank you."

"You're welcome."

He noticed her face had grown flushed, probably because he stood so near, but Titus didn't back away. If Savannah wasn't sitting nearby, he'd hold her, stroke his fingers down her cheeks and then tell her how much he appreciated everything she'd done for Savannah, everything she'd done for him. And he wasn't merely talking about the meal. She'd brightened one of the darkest times of his life, and he'd be forever grateful. But since Savannah was nearby and watching them intently, Titus had to keep a tight hold on the temptation to convert this act of friendship into something more, into the type of thing he'd have shared with a wife. He maintained the hint of distance between them and simply said, "Okay, are we ready to eat?"

Throughout the dinner, Isabella listened to Savannah describe their day, from role-playing sessions with her dolls to rearranging the plastic furniture in the backyard playhouse to deciding what they would cook for dinner. And with each animated observation from the six-year-old, Isabella knew with certainty that she'd never been a part of a real family.

Not at any point growing up. And certainly at no point during her marriage with Richard.

"And then I told Miss Isabella that we could make some chicken, but then we looked in the refrigerator, and we didn't have any chicken there! We just had this..." She held up her fork with a bit of roast on the end. "So that's what we made."

Savannah listed every detail with complete accuracy and without a hint of exaggeration. Obviously, she'd been taught that it was important to tell the truth, and not merely a portion of it...like Isabella had done when she hadn't told Titus the real reason she'd come to Claremont.

Throughout the day, as she spent time with Savannah and Titus and found how much she enjoyed being a small part of their world, she couldn't stop the feeling of deceitfulness consuming her soul. It didn't help that Brother Henry's lesson this morning had been about Luke 16 and the parable of the dishonest manager. The preacher had expressed Christ's value on honesty. Isabella knew Brother Henry couldn't possibly know her situation, but even so, his lesson couldn't have hit the mark any better. He hadn't merely stepped on her toes—he'd smashed them. And she knew God meant for her to get the message.

She had to tell Titus the truth.

"Can Miss Isabella come, too?" Savannah's question pulled her out of her thoughts.

"I'm sorry," she said, "come where?"

"To tuck me in for bed," Savannah said. "You want to, don't you?" She'd finished her cookies and milk while Isabella wasn't paying attention.

"Oh, yes, of course," Isabella said, glancing at Titus, "if that's okay with you."

He flinched, only a subtle reaction, but Isabella didn't miss his hesitation. Then he looked at Savannah and said, "I know it'd mean a lot to Savannah."

Isabella suspected that this had been a nightly tradition performed with Nan before she left. She'd already spent the entire day with them; maybe tucking Savannah in would qualify as overstaying her welcome. But Savannah had already accepted her answer as a yes.

"I'll go ahead and brush my teeth, so I'll be ready for y'all to tuck me in," she said, putting the last of her dishes in the sink and then hurrying up the stairs.

Isabella waited until she heard the water running in the upstairs bathroom, then said, "I probably shouldn't have stayed so long."

"No, I'm glad you did." He shook his head and sighed. "If I don't seem grateful, I'm sorry. I am. Really. It just surprised me when she asked you to help tuck her in." He didn't say anything else, but his tone told Isabella her suspicions were true.

"That was something y'all did as a family, wasn't it? You, Nan and Savannah?"

"I don't know why I even thought about it, after how long it's been." He glanced toward the front of the house. "I guess that box, and not knowing what's in it, has my mind wondering about things. But it isn't you. I think it's great that Savannah is opening up to you, and if she wants you to help tuck her in, then that's what I want, too." He smiled, but it looked unnatural and strained.

"I'm not sure—"

"I'm ready!" Savannah yelled.

He pointed toward the set of stairs Savannah had taken from the kitchen. "Come on," he said, his smile more genuine this time. "Ladies first."

She didn't know how to decline, so she

started up the stairs with Titus following. At
the top of the stairs, she noticed three rooms
that branched off of this end of the hallway.
She and Savannah had taken the front stairs
each time they'd gone to Savannah's room
during the day, so she hadn't yet seen this portion of the home. All three doors were open.
The one on the left was obviously the master,
with a huge four-poster canopied bed in its
center and complementing antique dressers
and nightstands. The floor, like the remainder
of the house, was hardwood, and the ceiling
was composed of hardwood planks, reminis-
cent of a church ceiling. The stained glass
windows, intricately colored and patterned
to resemble wisteria blooms, only added to
the stunning uniqueness of the room.

Because of the angle of the door to the second room, she only viewed one wall, lined
with boxes labeled Christmas Decorations,
Thanksgiving Decorations, and so on. A large
empty space in the middle matched the size
of a box marked Fourth of July Decorations
that sat in the center of the floor.

The third room was obviously the laundry
room, with a washer, a dryer and an ironing
board that currently held an assortment of

folded clothes, some of Savannah's and some of Titus's. Another two baskets of clothes sat on the floor near the washer.

"You'll have to forgive this part of the house," he said. "I do well to keep the downstairs picked up and clean. This is the portion that often gets neglected."

Isabella didn't see it that way at all. "I think it looks fine," she said honestly. In fact, if she and Savannah had wandered back here today, she'd have finished up the laundry for him and put the folded clothes away. She'd been impressed with how well the kitchen was stocked and organized, particularly for a single dad. Now she saw another glimpse into everything he'd had to do since Nan left. Laundry. Holiday decorating. Everything to keep his household running on his own.

Her admiration grew even more, as did her desire to come clean and tell him the truth.

"Are y'all coming?" Savannah called from the other end of the hall.

Titus laughed. "Miss Impatient," he said, "we're almost there."

Isabella still hadn't put her shoes on, and the hardwood floor seemed cooler against her feet than it had earlier in the day. Even so, the house radiated the natural warmth of an older home, a house that'd known many years of familial love. She suspected this was probably the least inhabited the home had ever been, and she thought of the massive master bedroom at the other end of the hall. And the fact that Titus had been sleeping there alone for three years, waiting to see if his wife would ever return.

Her heart thudded in her chest. He'd been hurt enough, and she hated that telling him the truth would hurt him again. But she didn't see any other way. And she still didn't know how to tell him that Nan had professed her love for him but never mentioned their little girl.

They entered Savannah's room to find her already snuggled under the covers. She smiled broadly when they entered. "I'm ready to say my prayers."

Titus moved ahead of Isabella to kneel near Savannah's head. He motioned to the spot next to him, and she followed his lead, kneeling beside him. Savannah, still smiling, patted Isabella's arm before closing her eyes.

"Dear God," she said, "thank You for letting me go to church today with Rose and

Daisy and for letting me make the sailboat in Sunday school and for me learning about Peter, James and John in the sailboat and for letting us have a good lunch with brownies and strawberries and for letting Miss Isabella come play with me and for letting us cook dinner. And God please bless Daddy and please bless Miss Isabella and please bless Mommy in heaven. Amen."

She opened her eyes and looked to Titus. "Your turn."

"Your prayer was perfect for both of us," he said, and kissed her forehead.

Her brow furrowed, mouth slid to the side, and Isabella suspected he'd been telling her that each night for a while now. However, Savannah, undeterred, turned her attention to the other adult in the room. "Your turn, Miss Isabella?"

There was no way Isabella could deny her request. So she closed her eyes and prayed, "Dear God, thank You for every blessing You've given me. Thank You for letting me spend the day here with Titus and Savannah. And please bless them, Lord. Take care of them and watch over them always. And be with me, too, Lord," she said, then silently added, *Help me do the right thing.* She swallowed, and then finished, "In Jesus' name, amen."

"That was a good one," Savannah said.

Isabella smiled. "Thanks."

Then Savannah opened her arms to her daddy. "Hugs and kisses."

He hugged her tightly and kissed her cheek. "Sweet dreams," he said, then moved away from the bed.

Savannah didn't miss a beat. She opened her arms again. "Hugs and kisses, Miss Isabella."

Isabella melted into her embrace, inhaled the sweet scent of Savannah's shampoo as their cheeks touched and as Isabella grasped the flood of emotions resulting from this little girl's hug.

"We had a great day, didn't we?" Savannah asked.

It took Isabella several blinks and a tough swallow to answer, but somehow she managed. "A great day," she said.

Savannah released her and then pulled the sheet up to her neck. "Can't wait to see what my hair looks like in the morning." She touched the braid that fell over her shoulder.

"It's going to be so pretty," Isabella said. "I can't wait to see it, too."

Savannah's mouth stretched open in a yawn. "Night," she whispered, then took a deep breath and closed her eyes, a smile still lifting her cheeks.

Titus turned out the light beside the bed, which caused a daisy night-light to illuminate at an outlet near the door. Then he pointed toward the hallway, and Isabella followed the silent instruction to leave Savannah's room.

Instead of walking toward the back of the house, Titus led her to the front stairs, so that they ended up in the foyer, where the box still sat on the table.

Titus paused, stared at it for a moment and moved toward it. Isabella held her breath as she prepared for him to see what Nan had sent, but instead of opening the box, he picked it up and carried it to a closet nearby.

"I should have done this when it first came," he said, sliding it onto a shelf above the coats. "I've made my decision. I don't want or need to know what's inside. Seeing it every day will only remind me of things I don't want to remember."

She watched as he shut the closet door and

then turned to face her, and she could almost see the weight of the box's presence lifted from his shoulders. The memory of Nan's abandonment hurt. The knowledge of her death hurt even more.

But Isabella knew that Nan had loved Titus. She'd professed her love for him, her mistake in leaving him, for months before she died. Her last words had been about him, asking Isabella to promise to find him and tell him that she'd never stopped loving him.

Isabella hadn't kept that promise. Not yet. But she would.

"Did you need to leave, or would you like to stay awhile?" he asked, obviously ready to take the subject off Nan's box. "We could sit on the porch if you want. The sun's already set, but I usually have a nice view of the stars above the mountain if the night's clear."

"I'd planned to clean up in the kitchen before I leave." She and Savannah had gone through several pots and pans, and then there were all of the plates and serving dishes that needed to be taken care of. She didn't want to leave him with that mess.

He grinned. "It doesn't work that way."

"What doesn't work that way?"

"I was raised to know that if a lady did the cooking, the fellow did the cleaning. My mom always cooked. Pops always cleaned." He opened the screen door leading to the porch. "So I'll clean the kitchen after you leave. We can sit and enjoy the night sky now."

She noticed he no longer gave her the option of leaving, which was good, because she wasn't ready to go. She needed to talk to him about Nan first. "I've never heard that rule," she said, "but I suppose it'd be futile to argue with it."

"Definitely." He remained at the door as she went through, the narrow opening causing her to brush against him as she passed.

Isabella liked being near him, liked getting to know him and all of his wonderful qualities. A guy who took great care of his little girl, who kept his home clean and kitchen well stocked for meals, who did the laundry and decorated for holidays. And who didn't allow a woman who cooked to clean the dishes.

Until the past couple of weeks, Isabella hadn't realized guys like Titus Jameson existed, except for the fact that Nan had told her he was like this. Nan had said he was amazing. And that she still loved him dearly.

Isabella gathered the courage needed to say the words on the tip of her tongue. *I knew your wife.* A perfect way to start the conversation. But she couldn't make her mouth form the sentence. Instead, she felt she was going to be sick.

"I appreciate you bringing Savannah home today," he said, as they took their seats on the porch swing. "I've never sent her to church without me, but—" he shook his head "—I've never wanted to be one of those hypocritical folks that goes to church because it's the thing to do and not because you felt like worshipping. I couldn't pull off worshipping today."

He didn't look at her, but stared toward the inky outline of the mountains beneath the moonlight. Stars dotted the blackness, and Isabella wondered if he saw the beautiful display the same way she did, as God's way of giving them a stunning backdrop for a difficult conversation.

Isabella had been trying to get the nerve to tell him about Nan, but obviously God was opening a different door here, and she'd follow His direction. "It's hard not to blame Him when times are tough."

Titus gently pushed them back and forth on the swing as he spoke. "It isn't that I blame Him," he said. "I don't think it's His fault that she left or that she died. But I can't help thinking there would've been some way to soften both blows. Or to help me to understand what happened, and not merely for me, but for Savannah. One day, she's going to start dating and thinking about relationships, and I know she's going to wonder what went wrong with her parents." He shook his head. "And I don't have a thing that I can tell her."

Again, Isabella sensed God opening a door and possibly giving her another means for letting Titus know how Nan felt about him when she died. She'd promised Nan she would tell Titus that she'd messed up in leaving him and that she'd never stopped loving him. But what if there was a way that Isabella didn't have to tell him herself? What if Nan could tell him?

She thought about the box now in the closet and all of the possibilities for what it contained. Surely Nan would've left something that showed Titus she still loved him. And perhaps the box also held something to show him she still loved Savannah, too.

"Maybe you do have something you can tell Savannah," she said. "About what happened, and about why Nan left."

He stopped pushing the swing and turned toward Isabella. "How would I have that?"

"Nan's box," she said, feeling more and more certain that her theory was correct. "Don't you think she left some information, maybe a note or a picture or something, that would give you a hint of how she was feeling when she left, or how she was feeling when she died? Maybe she regretted leaving you and Savannah, and maybe there's something in that box that lets you know."

"Or maybe she left us for someone else, and that guy abandoned ship when she got sick," he said quickly. Too quickly. As though this theory had been on his mind all along.

Isabella really thought he should open the box. She believed it'd help him, and she knew it'd help her. "Don't you think if there were someone else that Nan would've wanted a divorce?" She recalled the conversations she and Nan had had about her own divorce from Richard. Nan had acted as if she could relate, because of her relationship with her ex-husband. But now Isabella knew that she'd never had an ex-husband. She'd been married to Titus the entire time.

Isabella blinked past the pain of Nan's betrayal of her and prayed that there wasn't something in that box that actually enlightened Titus to a betrayal of him. She couldn't believe that Nan's professions of love on her deathbed were a lie. She wouldn't believe it. Nan may have lied about being married, but surely she hadn't lied about loving her husband. Isabella had sensed Nan's deep love for Titus, had been a little envious of it, truth be told. There was no way those confessions of love weren't true. "I think you should open it," she said.

When he remained silent, she thought he might be considering retrieving the box and opening it. Then she could be here to help him deal with the truth and accept the fact that Nan had never stopped loving him. She could help Nan get the message to him without conveying the fact that she'd befriended his wife before she died. But then he asked her a question that destroyed that theory completely.

"Have you ever had something that you

felt you should do, that seemed like the right thing to do, but you knew deep in your soul that following through would cause you— and other people you cared about—a whole lot of pain?"

Isabella thought of the past two weeks, and each day, hour and minute that she hadn't told him the truth. She nodded.

"Right," he said. "Well, that's how I feel about that box. Yeah, maybe I should open it and see what she left. But you've got to remember that the man at the hospital didn't even know I was her husband. He thought I was her brother. If there's anything in that box telling why she left me, then he'd have at least known I was in the picture, don't you think?"

She hadn't thought of that. "Maybe."

"Let me ask you something elsc. Did you follow through? Did you do whatever it was that you knew would hurt someone else? Say whatever you needed to say, do whatever you needed to do?"

Tough question. Easy answer. "No."

"Isabella," he said, "don't expect me to do something that you can't."

Chapter Eleven

I hope Savannah will forgive me.

"I placed the order for those bunk beds we found," Savvy said excitedly as she entered the trailer and bumped the door closed with her hip. "Dana said they have plenty of space at the dude ranch to store the furniture until the cabins are ready. But, according to Titus, as long as we don't have too much rain in July and August, the first one should be up and ready to furnish by September. We could potentially have children living here as early as October. Isn't that great?"

"Yes," Isabella said, mustering up a smile, "great."

Savvy's arms were filled with the furniture catalogs she and Isabella had picked up at the stores they'd visited last Friday, and she dropped them on Isabella's desk before sitting across from her, folding her arms and then raising one eyebrow in a look that said she expected more enthusiasm from her office manager.

"It *is* great," Isabella said, closing the file they'd received from the State Department of Family and Children Services of children needing placement. "Really. It'll be wonderful to tell kids that they have a nice place to live, a place where they'll be cared for and loved." She did her best to sound upbeat.

"Rose, Daisy and Savannah are out back playing on the swing set," Savvy said, still scrutinizing Isabella. "So you can spill now. No one's here but us. And I've waited long enough for you to fill me in voluntarily, so I'm asking, and I want to know. What's going on with you and Titus?"

Isabella had been expecting the question from Savvy all week, but they hadn't had a moment to themselves in the past four days, which had been fine with Isabella. She hadn't been ready to talk about the mess she'd caused on Sunday. But she was ready today.

She needed someone to confide in, someone to give her advice.

"On Sunday, when I took Savannah home, we had a wonderful time. I ended up staying and playing with her while Titus worked on repairing his porch railings. It was incredible, being there with them, sharing the day together. Savannah and I surprised Titus by fixing dinner for him, and we all ate together." She'd replayed the perfect scene over and over throughout the week, not only in her waking moments but also when she dreamed. That meal had obviously been nice for Titus, because it was a surprise. But it had meant plenty to Isabella, too, because it gave her a glimpse of what it'd be like if her dreams came true. However, after she returned to the B and B, reality set in. She'd felt the same way when she met Richard, as if her dreams had come true, and that had ended up as a nightmare.

Savvy's hand moved to her heart. "Oh, Isabella, that sounds like a perfect day."

Isabella didn't even need her past with Richard to make her realize that she could never have anything beyond friendship with

Titus. Because everything he knew about her was based on a lie.

"The day was good," she admitted, then recalled what started the downward spiral. "But, that night, Savannah asked me to help tuck her in, and apparently that was something that they'd always done together—Nan, Titus and Savannah."

Savvy frowned. "Brought back memories for him?"

"Yes, and we started talking about what had happened back then, and he mentioned how he would never know why Nan left." She recalled the awkward conversation on the porch swing. "I suggested that he should open the box of her things that the hospital sent, because there might be something in there that would let him know why she left, maybe even let him know that she'd still loved him all along."

"Titus got a box? Of Nan's things?" Savvy asked. "And he hasn't opened it?"

"He *won't* open it. I think he believes whatever is inside will convince him that she never loved him the way he thought she did."

"Oh, my," Savvy said, "bless Titus's heart. I know that has to be tough, but he needs to open it. How will he ever have closure if he doesn't?"

"That's what I think, too, so I told him he should," Isabella said, "and he's barely spoken to me since."

"So *that's* what's been going on with you two," Savvy said, leaning back in the chair and chewing on her lower lip. She sat there for a moment while Isabella prayed that she'd give her some advice she could work with. She didn't want a relationship with Titus, but she hadn't intended on losing the friendship. Then Savvy straightened and said, "He has to open that box. That's all there is to it."

Obviously, *that* bit of wisdom wasn't going to cut it. "He won't. And there's more," Isabella said, needing to confess everything. "I haven't been honest with him. There's something I need to tell him, and I haven't." Odd, but merely saying even that much made her feel a little better.

Savvy nodded her head once, as if she'd expected this insight. "I know a thing or two about that, keeping secrets from each other, because Brodie and I were both guilty of it. We each had secrets in our past that we had no intention of sharing, not with anyone else and certainly not with each other, but until we did, our relationship was one big lie. You can't start a relationship with a lie. It never works."

Now *that* was the kind of advice Isabella had expected. And what she needed to hear. Until she told Titus about Nan, a relationship—even if that meant a friendship only—would never be a possibility. "I need to tell him the truth, but how can I when we're barely speaking?"

"You're still giving Savannah swim lessons each afternoon, right?"

"Yes, but he doesn't say any more than necessary, the same way he does every morning when he drops Savannah off at the trailer. And we'll have our last lesson for this week today, since tomorrow is the Fourth of July. I probably won't even see him again until Monday."

Savvy waved her hand dismissively. "Are you kidding? You'll see him at every Fourth of July event tomorrow. We've got the softball game, then the parade and then the fireworks, and you'll go to all of them, and you'll make sure to spend time with him."

"I hadn't planned to go." She'd heard enough

about the activities to know the town offered them each year, but it also sounded like a family affair.

She had no family.

"You're going," Savvy said, not offering no as an option. "And tomorrow, you'll make him talk to you. Tell him that you need to tell him the truth, and then tell him whatever it is. You'll feel better for it, and I'm sure he will, too."

"Make him talk to me," Isabella repeated, dumbfounded. "How?"

Savvy shook her head in apparent disbelief. "You really don't see the way he looks at you? Whether he wants to admit it or not, Titus Jameson has already started falling, and as much as he tries to stay away, if you tell him you want to talk, he'll listen."

"I'm not so sure," Isabella said, uncertain that he was falling for her—which she was pretty sure would never happen, since he was obviously still in love with Nan—and also that she could pull off making him listen.

"That's okay," Savvy said, grinning as she scooped up a few of the magazines she'd dropped on the desk. "You don't have to be sure. I'm sure enough for both of us. Tonight, you talk to him and tell him the truth. Tomorrow, we'll work on how you can convince him to open that box."

"I..." Isabella started.

"Will. That's the rest of your sentence," Savvy said with a grin. "I will."

"I will," Isabella repeated, and then silently added, *try.*

It didn't matter that he could no longer see the box. Ever since his conversation with Isabella Sunday night, Titus hadn't stopped thinking about it or wondering what was inside. And the more his curiosity increased, the more resolute he became in the belief that whatever Nan had left behind would do him in.

Part of him wanted to burn the thing. Or take it to the Claremont dump and toss it. Maybe drop it at the top of Jasper Falls and watch it plummet.

Another part wanted to rip it open and determine what had happened during her last three years.

Unfortunately, whatever he'd started feeling toward Isabella on Sunday had been hindered by his preoccupation with the box and by her insistence that he should open it. That box served as a reminder that the first woman he'd ever loved, the mother of his child, had abandoned him and Savannah. It reminded him that, even when she knew she was dying, Nan hadn't felt the need to let him know, hadn't thought he deserved a chance to tell her goodbye or to let them see her one more time. And it reminded him that people you care about—people you love—can leave without warning. Without explanation. With no regard to the shattered hearts left in their wake.

Yes, he'd started having feelings toward Isabella, but how did he know she wouldn't do the same thing? He'd believed he'd known Nan so well, and she'd blindsided him. How could he let himself fall so easily for someone that he'd just met? Titus wouldn't have thought it possible, but on Sunday, he'd sensed his heart tumbling for the beautiful, sensitive woman with the tormented past. And during the four days since, he'd done his best to reel it back in.

He'd seen Isabella each morning when he dropped Savannah off, and he'd thanked her for fixing her hair. He'd also spent each afternoon with her at the pool, but he kept his attention on Savannah and made no more comments to Isabella than absolutely necessary. When it was time to leave, he'd politely thank her and then gently coax Savannah away from the woman she undeniably loved.

Titus didn't want to harm the relationship Savannah had developed with Isabella, because he knew how much it helped her to have a mother figure in her life again. He just couldn't let himself see Isabella as someone to fill the huge void in his own world.

Quite honestly, he didn't know if he'd ever be ready to have that space filled again.

By the time Savannah's swim lesson ended Thursday afternoon, Titus believed he'd sufficiently distanced himself from Isabella. There was no way she hadn't noticed that their relationship was clearly friendship. Nothing more, nothing less. Even today, while he'd praised Savannah for her new skill of swimming underwater, he'd kept his attention off Isabella and focused solely on his daughter.

Thankfully, this would be their last swim lesson of the week, since tomorrow was the Fourth of July, and the entire town would be busy with the traditional festivities—a friendly community softball game in the morning, the parade in the afternoon and fireworks tomorrow evening. Granted, he'd probably see Isabella at some of the events, but there would be plenty of people around. They wouldn't be as isolated as they were now, with merely the two of them and Savannah at the pool.

"Did you see me, Daddy? Wasn't that awesome?" Savannah asked as she exited the water and accepted her towel from Titus.

"Very awesome," he said, while she dried off and Isabella, still in the pool, swam to the deep end to retrieve a couple of kickboards they'd used at the beginning of the lesson. He didn't want to watch how elegantly she moved when she swam, or the way her hair billowed behind her in the water, the red shimmering against the late-afternoon sun.

He didn't *want* to watch. But he couldn't help himself.

"Someday I want to swim that good, like Miss Isabella," Savannah said, obviously aware that her father gawked at the woman in the pool.

Titus turned away from the affecting image to gather Savannah's shorts and T-shirt from the table. "Here you go," he said. "Go ahead and get dressed, please." He wanted her to be ready to leave before Isabella came out of the water.

Savannah slipped her T-shirt over her head, stepped into her shorts and then caught sight of her friend at the barn. "Hey, there's Abi," she said, waving toward Abi, her parents Landon and Georgiana, as well as John and Dana, all standing near a blue horse trailer.

Abi waved back and yelled, "Savannah! Come see our new pony!"

"Oh, wow!" Savannah grabbed her shoes and pushed her feet inside. "Daddy, I'm going to go see the new pony, okay?"

Titus didn't have the option to say no. What reason could he give and, besides, Savannah had already started running toward the barn. "Just for a few minutes!" he yelled after her, and then thought he might head to the barn, too, at least until their swim instructor left.

But before he could start an exit, Isabella reached the steps and began climbing out. So instead of escaping to the barn, he did the gentlemanly thing, grabbing her beach towel from the table and meeting her as she reached the concrete. Her swimsuit today was a deep purple. The rich hue seemed to draw more attention to the reddish tones in her hair and the vivid green of her eyes.

"Thank you," she said, reaching toward the towel with her right hand and then extending the kickboards she clutched in her left. "Can you hold these while I dry off?"

"Sure," he said, taking the boards. But instead of standing there and watching her, which wouldn't do anything for distancing himself from his natural attraction, he walked back to the table, picked up her large beach bag and slid the boards inside. By the time he turned around, she'd finished drying, had already slid on a pair of shorts and was pulling an Atlanta Braves T-shirt over her head.

The additional clothing should have made him stop noticing how beautiful she was after she swam, but Isabella's attractiveness wasn't merely physical. She radiated inner beauty as well, from the way she smiled to the way she spoke to the way she studied her surroundings with those inquisitive green eyes.

Titus cleared his throat and prepared to tell her he was going to the barn. Anything to get away from the urge to push that wet lock of auburn hair away from her cheek. And to stop wondering what it'd feel like to hold her, kiss her or tell her that, in spite of his attempt to keep his distance, he hadn't stopped thinking about her all week.

"Kind of tough to avoid talking to me when it's just the two of us here, isn't it?" she asked, those green eyes studying him and making him feel as though she knew how very difficult it was to fight whatever he felt toward her. One corner of her mouth dipped down, and she looked troubled. "Titus, I need to apologize."

He had no idea what she had to feel sorry about. The problem wasn't with Isabella. It was with him. He'd simply realized he wasn't ready to trust a female again—didn't know if he'd ever be ready—and he'd let his feelings for Isabella and his gratitude for her helping Savannah teeter too close to the edge of love. Certainly, that wasn't her fault. "Apologize for what?"

"I obviously made you uncomfortable Sunday night when I told you that I thought you should open that box of Nan's things. You've hardly spoken to me all week, barely even looked at me," she said, her tone saying that both facts hurt. "And I want you to know that I'm sorry."

Titus didn't want to hurt her, but he also didn't want to put himself in the situation to be hurt again. Or risk Savannah getting hurt. Yet Savannah was already so emotionally connected to Isabella that if something happened to take her out of Savannah's life, Titus knew his little girl would be devastated.

Had he already messed up by letting them grow so close?

He looked toward the barn and saw Savannah and Abi petting the new pony while the adults took photos with their phones, which gave him some time to justify his actions this week. "I don't know any other way to explain this than to tell you the truth," he said.

"Okay." She stuffed her towel in the bag with the kickboards. "I'm listening."

Titus took a deep breath, let it out and decided to start with the basics. "Sunday spooked me."

Confusion etched clearly across her features. "Spooked you, how?"

"Having you there, with Savannah and with me, spending the day with us, playing with her and taking care of her, sharing din-

ner together and then tucking Savannah in."
He shook his head and wished he were better
with words. He was a guy, and guys weren't
all that great at sharing feelings. Nan had
often reminded him of that when they were
married. She'd also told him it was best to
simply put it all out there, say what he was
thinking instead of making her try to guess.
Typical females weren't into guessing the
feelings—or lack thereof—going on in a
guy's head.

But Isabella wasn't a typical female. She'd
been hurt growing up, had never had a real
family and had been through a sorry excuse
of a marriage. And on Sunday, he'd seen it
on her face; she'd felt something happening
between them, too. For Titus to act as though
he could give her whatever she wanted was
wrong. He couldn't. Because he couldn't get
over what happened with Nan. If he were over
it, it wouldn't have bothered him when Savannah asked Isabella to tuck her in, wouldn't
have stabbed his heart when she said he
should open that box.

"Letting me spend the day with you and
Savannah spooked you," she said quietly, "because it reminded you of what you had with

Nan and what you lost." She pushed her hands in the pockets of her shorts, looked toward the mountains as if deciding what to say next. Then her head moved in a subtle nod and she turned back to Titus.

Titus didn't know what to say.

She shook her head. "Think about what you had with her, Titus. The family that y'all had together with Savannah. Any woman who had something that wonderful wouldn't have left without a good reason." She closed her eyes for a moment, and Titus wondered if she were saying a quick prayer. Then she opened them and asked, "Don't you think that she may have left you something that tells you what that reason was? If you'd just open the box…"

He couldn't believe they were back to this again. Why wouldn't she leave it alone? "Nothing in that box is going to change the fact that she walked out, or that she died without giving us a chance to say goodbye." He wished he could control the anger in his tone, but he was done talking about that box, done thinking about it.

She shook her head, looked up at the sky and released a ragged breath. Titus didn't know why this had her so upset. It wasn't as if it were her problem—it was his. "Titus, I need to tell you something."

They'd been so intent on the conversation that they hadn't seen or heard the two girls sprinting toward the pool, with John and Dana following close behind.

"Daddy! I forgot to tell you about the bonfire!" Savannah yelled breathlessly.

He wanted to ask Isabella what she needed to say, but she'd turned her back when the girls neared, probably to keep them from seeing her so emotional. "Bonfire?" he asked.

"Tomorrow night. They told us at church, but I forgot to tell you."

"We're having a bonfire here for the kids," Dana explained, as she and John joined the girls by the pool. "Since so many of them get scared by the loud fireworks, we thought we'd do a kid thing at the ranch for the Fourth. We're going to roast marshmallows, make s'mores, sing songs."

"And spend the night!" Abi added.

"In tents!" Savannah said. "Isn't that great, Daddy?"

The thought of her spending the night outside in a tent didn't sit well with him. He asked Dana, "Is Savannah old enough for this thing?"

"I am, Daddy," she said. "Rose and Daisy are going to be here. And they're six, same as me."

But Titus awaited Dana's answer.

"We're actually starting at age five," she said. "Savannah had mentioned she wanted to come when we announced it during children's church on Sunday, so I'd already put her down to stay in the tent with Savvy, Rose and Daisy. We have an adult and three kids in each tent," she explained.

"And we'll spend the night and then we're going to ride horses and go fishing on Saturday," Savannah said excitedly.

"We're planning on the fun lasting until Saturday afternoon," John said. "And we'd love for Savannah to come, if that's okay with you."

Savannah had never spent the night away from home except for an occasional weekend trip to the beach with Titus's folks. "Are you sure you want to stay?" he asked. "All night?"

"Daddy, I'm six," she answered, as though that were the all-important I'm-growing-up number. And maybe it was.

"Okay, then, I guess that's fine," he said, and was rewarded with an exuberant hug from Savannah.

"Thanks so much, Daddy!"

He patted her back and got the details from Dana and John, all the while watching Isabella keep her back to them during the process of gathering her things.

She started walking toward her car without looking back, but her shaking shoulders and an occasional movement of her hand to her face told Titus she was crying. He wanted to check on her, ask her why she was so upset, but he didn't want to draw attention to the fact, since he seemed to be the only one who noticed. Everyone else chattered nonstop about the Fourth of July plans.

"I'll see all of you tomorrow," Isabella called, climbing in her car. She'd parked far enough away that Titus couldn't see her face, and neither could the remainder of the group.

"See you tomorrow!" Dana returned.

"Bye, Miss Isabella!" Savannah called.

Titus couldn't let her leave without finding out what she needed to tell him that had her so worked up. "Hang on. I'll be right back," he said to the group, then he sprinted to her car.

She was looking through her purse when he tapped on the driver's side window, and she jumped. Then she rubbed both palms across her cheeks and lowered the window.

Her long lashes were wet spikes, but Titus didn't think that was from swimming as much as from crying, and he hated that he'd made her cry. He leaned his forehead against the top of the door. "Isabella, what is it? Are you okay?"

She sniffed. "I will be."

He knew John and Dana were probably watching, but he didn't care. "You said you had something to talk to me about."

She leaned forward to look past him, presumably at the group still by the pool. "It can wait." Then she blinked through the tears and started the car. "I've got to go, Titus. Sorry I got so upset. I've got a lot on my mind." Then she rolled up the window and drove away, leaving Titus to wonder why, if he'd worked so hard to distance himself from her all week, he wanted nothing more than to run after her now.

Chapter Twelve

I hope you will forgive me, too.

Titus woke even earlier than usual Friday morning. Or rather, he never really went to sleep. His night had been filled with the memory of Isabella crying and then leaving. Their brief conversation, combined with how miserable he'd felt when she'd driven away, had convinced him that his plan to stay away from her would never work.

He couldn't get her off his mind, couldn't get her out of his heart. But she was convinced that he needed to open that box and see what Nan had left behind, and Titus had realized this week, as he tried to stay away from Isabella and then failed, that she was probably right. Unless he opened—and closed—that final chapter of his relationship with Nan, he'd never be able to move forward with anyone, even someone as amazing as Isabella Gray.

But the memory of the day Nan walked out and the moment when he read that single sheet of paper that ended up being her final letter cut so deeply that Titus didn't know if he could handle another stab of pain regarding the marriage he'd thought would last forever.

So he *still* hadn't opened the box. And he *still* wasn't ready to move on.

He needed advice, and he knew where to get it.

As the first rays of sunlight pierced the sky, Titus finished off his second cup of coffee, placed the cup on the porch table and picked up his phone. Unlike his mother, Titus's father never slept past sunup. Right now, he was probably on his back deck watching it rise above the gulf. A perfect time for the two of them to have a heart-to-heart while the ladies of their lives, Titus's mother and Savannah, were still sleeping.

He selected the number from his Favorites, and his father answered after the first ring.

Titus heard him clearing his throat, and then he answered, "Hey, son, what's wrong?"

His dad knew him well. "You're saying I only call when something's wrong?"

"Usually, but there's nothing terrible about that," his dad said. "So, does this have something to do with Isabella?"

Titus shook his head, not overly surprised that his mother had already filled him in on the little tidbit she'd assumed when they talked last week. Turned out her assumption, as usual, was pretty close to the mark. "Mom told you about Isabella?"

"Just that she's new to Claremont, that Savannah loves her and that she's pretty sure God sent her to you because she prayed for Him to. Nothing much more than that," he said, humor lining every word.

Titus laughed. "It's a good thing I love her."

"Can't help but love her, that's what I always say," his father said, also chuckling. "So...*is* this about Isabella?"

"Partly," Titus admitted. "And it's also about Nan."

A thick inhalation echoed through the line, then his father let it out in a whoosh and said, "Okay, I'm ready. Shoot."

Titus pictured his dad seated on the back deck and closing his eyes the way he did when he wanted to fully concentrate on what someone said. He'd never appreciated his father's ability for objective analysis more than now. So he thought through the important aspects of what was going on in his life and started with, "The hospital where Nan died sent a box of her things."

"Okay," his dad said slowly, "and I take it that something in that box disturbed you."

Titus frowned. "I have no idea. I haven't opened it."

Silence echoed through the line, and he could almost see his father nodding, putting the pieces together and knowing Titus well enough that he probably knew why that box was still sealed.

"Afraid of what's inside?" he finally asked.

The sun crept higher, the brilliant light somehow adding even more intensity to his father's question. "That's pretty much it."

"And until you know what's in that box, and what really happened with Nan, you can't move forward with this Isabella, who, according to your mother, is perfect for you." He made the last part of the statement with another hint of humor.

"Kind of hard for her to determine, don't you think, since she's never met Isabella," Titus said.

"Yeah, but you know your mom. She gets it in her head that something's a certain way, and nothing shakes that."

"She'd also been certain Nan was coming back, Dad," Titus reminded him. In fact, his mother hadn't given up on Nan returning until well past the second year.

His father heaved a sigh. "I think deep down she knew Nan wasn't coming back, but she just hated seeing you and Savannah hurt so badly."

"I know." Titus appreciated the depth of his mother's love but also needed advice from the parent that wouldn't sugarcoat the truth. "But Nan didn't come back, and now I may have a chance to find out why."

"I see." His father did see, Titus was certain, and probably already knew how he would handle this situation, which was the whole reason Titus had called. He needed someone to tell him what he already knew in his heart.

"So what would you do?" he asked.

"You don't really have a choice, do you? If you want to move forward—and you and I both know that you can't stay stuck in the past and live a productive life—then you've got to open that box, deal with whatever is inside and move ahead. Maybe with Isabella, if your mother's intuition is still alive and well."

"That's what I thought you'd say," Titus admitted.

"And, of course, you should pray. You are keeping God in this equation, aren't you?"

This time, the silence that echoed through the line came from Titus.

His dad gave him a couple of beats to answer, and when he didn't, he said, "Don't give up on Him, son. You need Him now, whether you realize it or not."

Titus had the answer he'd wanted to gain from this conversation, and he didn't want to get into a faith discussion with his dad. "Nan wasn't the only one who let me down, Dad."

"Titus…"

"But I appreciate the advice. Tell Mom I said Happy Fourth."

"Take the advice, son, and not merely the part about opening the box," his father said. "And Happy Fourth to you, too."

Titus disconnected and continued watching the sun rise, bathing Main Street and bringing attention to the red, white and blue bunting decorating each of the antebellum homes, his included. Though he wasn't ready to take all of his father's advice yet, he would take care of the one thing causing him the most grief. Nan's box. Before the day ended, he'd find out what was inside and deal with it. Today was Independence Day, after all. Time to say goodbye to the things of the past and maybe, just maybe, say hello to the future.

"About time you decided to show up," Savvy said, as Isabella climbed the bleachers at the Hydrangea Park baseball field. "I saved you a seat, but I was about to think you weren't going to need it."

Isabella knew the seat was saved, since Savvy had included that in one of the many text messages she'd sent over the past hour and a half.

"You didn't forget about the game, did you?" Savvy asked.

Saying hello to the other people she knew in the stands, Isabella continued weaving through the seated spectators on her way to get to Savvy, who'd selected a spot in the center of the top row. She held up her phone as she neared her friend. "How could I? You've been texting me nonstop since it started."

Savvy, as well as everyone seated around her, laughed. "Well, it took you long enough. This is the last bat of the last inning."

Isabella could remind her that her texts had focused more on one particular player than on the actual game.

Titus is here.

He's scanning the stands. I think he's looking for you.

He just hit a triple, and YOU MISSED IT.

Savannah wants you to braid her hair. I could do it, but she's asking for you.

You missed him hitting a double this time.

And then the last text, the one that caused Isabella to finally get in the car and drive to Hydrangea Park.

Get here now!

Isabella wedged into the tiny space Savvy had saved between her and Dana. "Where are all of the kids?"

"Over there, on the playground," Savvy said, pointing toward the children's area in the center of all the fields without taking her eyes off the guy coming up to bat. "I've gotta say, there's something about a man in uniform."

Dana giggled. "You've been saying it every time Brodie comes up to bat."

"Hey, I feel the same way when I watch him bat now as I did every time he batted in high school. Still makes my heart race." She whistled loudly, the sound so shrill that Isabella winced, and then she yelled, "You've got this, babe!"

He grinned and winked at his wife, which caused her to whistle again and earn another round of laughs from those seated around her in the stands.

Isabella had known she'd feel out of place at the game. As she suspected, the bleachers were filled with couples cheering on the local team, or with the wives and girlfriends of the guys on the field. Plus, she had no idea whether Titus would want her here watching or not, in spite of the fact that Savvy seemed convinced he was looking for her.

Yesterday, she'd tried to follow Savvy's advice and tell him the truth about knowing Nan. But then she'd messed up, making him angry when she mentioned Nan's things again. She should have told him the truth and forgotten about the box. Then maybe they could have dealt with it and moved past it.

Or maybe he'd have gotten even angrier and told her he never wanted to see her again.

"Here comes your guy," Savvy whispered in her ear, as Titus moved from the dugout to the warm-up circle.

"He isn't my guy," Isabella said, but she couldn't take her eyes off him, wearing a crimson-and-gray Claremont baseball jersey and white baseball pants. Though she wouldn't verbalize it, she totally agreed with Savvy. There was *something* about a man in uniform.

He took a couple of swings with the bat and then stopped, pivoted toward the stands…and looked directly at Isabella. He had a swipe of black beneath each eye and a bit more of a beard shadow than she'd ever noticed before, making him look ruggedly handsome and undeniably masculine. Startled, she held up her hand and waved her fingers. He nodded, grinned and sent her heart into overdrive.

"He's *not* your guy?" Savvy continued, thankfully still at a whisper.

"I didn't tell him," Isabella whispered back.

"Didn't tell him what?"

"The truth," she said. "That secret I told you about."

Still staring at the field, probably since Brodie was hanging off third and contemplating stealing home, Savvy frowned. "Well, you have got to take care of that today. There's something going on between you two, and you need to get those old problems out of the way so you can make this thing work. He's too good of a catch for you to miss out on." Then she shoved Isabella's shoulder with hers. "And you're too good of a catch for him to miss out on, too."

"He may not want to catch me once I tell him," Isabella mumbled, tired of denying the truth that kept staring her in the face and kicking her in the heart. As much as she fought it and as much as she wanted to keep her guard up after what had happened with Richard, each and every time she was around Titus Jameson, she realized how very opposite he was to her ex. And how amazing it'd be to be on the receiving end of his love.

No longer paying attention to anything beyond the game, Savvy didn't hear her comment. "If he knocks Brodie in, we'll win. We haven't beaten the Stockville team in three years, and we're about to do it now." She yelled, "Come on, Titus! You've got this. Bring Brodie in!"

Isabella also watched the man at the plate, the bat held high and his stance quite impressive. The baseball uniform did do amazing things to his fit physique. His back muscles, usually displayed in the soft cotton of his work shirt, were even more prominent in the jersey fabric. She watched as his hands opened and closed around the bat as he got a better grip and prepared for the pitch, and she recalled how capable those hands were at handling wood, a hammer, nails…and at hugging his little girl.

And even when she'd warned her heart that there could never be anything between them beyond friendship, she'd still found herself wondering several times over the past week what it'd feel like to be in those arms.

The first two pitches were balls, and Savvy was none too happy about it. "Come on! Throw him something he can hit!"

Though the pitcher didn't seem to notice her, Titus stepped out of the batter's box, looked to the stands and grinned. Then he stepped back into the box and waited for the next pitch.

"Yell something for him," Savvy urged.

Isabella had never been the type to yell at a ball game. Richard would have thought she'd gone crazy to act that way in public. But she did want to encourage him now, so she cupped her hands and yelled, "You can do it, Titus!"

And she saw his shoulders lift, watched his hands open and flex around the bat again, and knew that he'd actually heard her cheering him on. Then the pitcher threw the ball and the crack of the bat hitting it was earsplitting, as was the sound of the crowd cheering as the ball soared over center field toward the pine trees well beyond the fence.

"Home run!" the announcer called over the crackly PA system. "Claremont wins!"

Savvy grabbed Isabella in a hug that nearly took her breath away. "See what happens when you yell for your man!" Then she started down the stands to find Brodie, laughing and high-fiving the other guys on the team, and all of them clapping Titus on the back as he crossed home plate or shoving him the way guys do when they've gained a victory.

The stands cleared out as the townsfolk went down to congratulate the team, and she followed suit. She didn't want to stand there by herself, but she also wasn't certain about the appropriate thing for her to do or say to Titus. As she'd told Savvy, Titus wasn't her guy, and she was pretty sure she'd made him angry yesterday. And then there was the fact that she'd been crying when she left him last night, and she hadn't told him why.

He might not even want her to say anything to him now.

That notion disintegrated when he left the team and headed directly toward Isabella.

"Thanks for coming," he said, then grinned, "and for yelling."

"I had no idea what to yell," she said, then shrugged at how peculiar that sounded. "I've never yelled at ball games."

He laughed. "It doesn't matter what you yell. What matters is that you're heard by the team." He pulled at the Velcro on his batting glove, yanked it off and stuffed it in his back pocket.

She hadn't been yelling for the team. She'd been yelling for him specifically, but she was grateful he didn't choose to point that out. "It was a good game," she said.

"Yes, it was, even if you only saw the end of the last inning."

Isabella swallowed. How would he know that if he *hadn't* been looking for her in the stands? Savvy had been right.

He removed his hat, wiped at the dust on his forehead with the back of his hand and then slid it back on. "Why was that? Why'd you wait until the end?"

Isabella had promised herself that she would no longer lie to him, and she'd start keeping that promise right now. "I wasn't sure you'd want me here."

He took a step closer. "Well, I do," he said, his voice low and gravelly. "I didn't think you'd come after last night, with me making you cry, but I'm glad you did."

"I'm glad I did, too." Very glad, in fact.

"I need to apologize for getting mad when you mentioned that box of Nan's things. I wasn't ready to talk about it, wasn't ready to think about it, and I took that out on you. I'm sorry."

"I shouldn't have mentioned it again," she said.

"Good game, Titus," John Cutter said as he and Dana passed nearby.

"Thanks. You, too," Titus said, then waited until they were out of earshot before saying, "the thing is, you were right. The only way I'll ever have any chance of knowing what happened three years ago is to open that box."

Isabella couldn't believe what she was hearing. "You've decided to open it?"

"I have," he said, "but I haven't done it yet. I don't want to do it when Savannah's at home, don't want to risk her seeing something that might upset her..." He let the word hang, and Isabella thought she knew why.

"And you don't want her to see you get upset," she guessed.

"The truth is, I don't know what Nan left

behind. It could be something that tells me exactly why she left, or it could tell me nothing." He shrugged. "Just in case it's something that doesn't sit well, I'd rather her not be around for that revelation."

Isabella nodded, impressed at how he always put Savannah first. "So when are you going to open it?"

"Tonight, after I drop her off at the dude ranch to spend the night."

"I'll pray that everything goes well." She'd also pray that Nan did leave something behind to let him know that she loved him and hopefully that she loved Savannah, too. Then maybe Isabella would never have to tell him that she'd withheld the truth about his wife.

His jaw tensed. "You can pray if you want to," he said, reminding her that he still wasn't all that keen on God at the moment, "but there's something else that you can do, too, something that would mean a lot to me."

"What is it?" she asked.

"You could be there when I open it."

Memories of Nan rushed in with a vengeance. Nan, talking about her ex-husband and how much she loved him. Nan, telling

Isabella about the mistake she'd made when she'd walked out on him. And then Nan, knowing she was dying and asking Isabella to find Titus and tell him how very much she cared. If Isabella was with him when he opened that box, she'd have to go through all of those emotions again, losing her dear friend again. "I'm not sure I should be there."

"Isabella, I haven't told anyone else in town about it. No one knows how much this thing has been haunting me ever since it arrived at my door last week except you." He moved a little closer. "And I want you there."

"I don't understand why." Why would he need to have her there when it had nothing to do with her? This was about Nan, and he didn't know that Isabella had a relationship with her, too. Or did he? "Why would you want me there?" she asked, trying to keep the anxiety out of her tone. Surely he hadn't learned the truth.

"Because you're a big part of the reason I want to close the door on my past," he said.

She blinked, surprised at his answer. "I am?"

He touched his finger to her chin, his

mouth lifting in a smile that sent a tremor all the way to her soul. "I can't move forward until I close the door on the past."

Isabella thought he might kiss her here, by the baseball field with almost everyone in Claremont watching, and right now, she didn't see a thing in the world wrong with that. But then he moved his finger away and pointed behind her.

"Get ready," he said, "she's been waiting to see you all morning."

She turned to see Savannah sprinting toward them, her knees dirty from the playground and her smile absolutely contagious. Or maybe Isabella really, really wanted to smile. Because she found herself practically beaming at the little girl headed their way.

"Miss Isabella! I need you to fix this, because Daddy left it *so* messy." She pointed to the pitiful ponytail, uncaptured strands sticking out in several directions and clumps of hair protruding on the top of her head.

"It isn't too bad," she said, which would probably count as a lie, and the look on Titus's face said he knew it, "but I think I can make it a little better."

"The bar isn't that high," Titus said, laughing, and Isabella laughed, too. It felt great to be beside him and with the two of them again.

It felt right.

"Here's my brush and stuff," Savannah said, handing over the small pink bag that she seemed to carry everywhere.

Isabella had the messy ponytail taken down in no time at all, and then she worked to ease the brush through the tangles, gather Savannah's hair neatly at her crown and contain it with a pink hair band that matched her T-shirt.

"I like it when you fix my hair," Savannah said, hugging Isabella.

Isabella always loved receiving a hug from Savannah, but this one felt even better than usual, because of Titus, looking at her as though he were ready to move forward. And maybe because he was ready to move forward…with her. Maybe there was a place for her in his and Savannah's world and maybe that place went beyond friendship.

Was she ready for that? Could she trust him not to hurt her the way Richard had?

She glanced up to see Titus looking at her with so much compassion and understanding.

He knew about her past, and he didn't think he needed to change her because of it, didn't think that she had anything to be ashamed of because she hadn't had a family.

And with Titus and Savannah, Isabella had learned, truly learned, what it'd feel like to be a part of a real family.

Yes, she realized, she was ready—very ready—for that.

"Thanks, Miss Isabella," Savannah said, still hugging her tightly.

"You're welcome," she said, emotions causing the words to come out raspy and raw.

Though she knew Titus noticed, Savannah obviously didn't.

"Isn't this day great?" she asked. "The next thing is the parade and then I get to go to the bonfire and spend the night with my friends. The parade comes right by our house after lunch. You want to come watch it with me and Daddy? Rose and Daisy are gonna watch it there, and some other people, too. You wanna come?" she repeated.

Isabella looked to Titus, who nodded.

Please, he mouthed.

Her week had taken a marvelous turn for the better, and she said a quick but heartfelt prayer of thanks. "I'd love to."

Chapter Thirteen

True love brings happiness, more joy than I'd have thought possible.

"Miss Isabella, look, it's the football team! They're always the last ones, and they always have lots of candy!" Savannah yelled.

The flatbed truck, decorated with the red, white and blue similar to the preceding vehicles in the parade, eased toward them on Main Street. Isabella heard some of the boys on the truck yelling to the crowd, but she could barely make out their words because the band had just passed, and the booming from the drums still reverberated in her ears.

"Look, there's Dylan!" Rose and Daisy yelled, jumping up and down and waving their arms to get their big brother's attention. "Dylan, throw us some candy!"

Dylan, wearing his football jersey like all of the other guys, pointed to the group and then encouraged his teammates to toss them plenty of treats. Sure enough, a bombing of Jolly Ranchers and bubble gum and other candies, tossed exuberantly by the Claremont High School football team, cascaded over all of them as they laughed. Savannah, Rose, Daisy and Abi alternated between scooping up the candy and stuffing it in their mouths.

Isabella couldn't remember the last time she'd had this much fun. Throughout the day, she'd learned that this was an annual ritual, the group gathering at Titus's house to share a picnic lunch and then watch the parade. The lunch had been fabulous, with everyone bringing something to share. Titus grilled hamburgers and hot dogs, and all of his friends—Isabella's friends, too, she realized—brought the sides, potato salad, deviled eggs, chips and a wide assortment of desserts that included homemade ice cream and chocolate chip cookies.

She'd felt good that she'd picked up a fruit tray from the local grocery before she arrived. It'd been something Richard had instilled in her, never to arrive at any gathering without bringing something to the host. But Titus shook his head when she walked in with the tray. "I didn't mean for you to bring anything," he said. "You're still a guest around here."

She'd smiled, handed over the tray and thought how she didn't want to be a guest anymore. If he was really thinking about moving forward, she wanted to be a part of it. She wanted to be a part of this, and not merely on special occasions and holidays, but always. She wanted to be a part of Titus's and Savannah's life.

Titus and Brodie had walked to the front of the flatbed truck to say something to the driver, apparently another friend of theirs. Isabella watched Titus chat with the guy and laugh at something Brodie said, then turn and walk back toward her.

Savvy's words from this morning continued to tease her thoughts.

Here comes your guy.

"What's that about?" he asked as he neared.

"What's what about?"

"That smile," he said, tilting his head toward her face. "And that look, like you've got a secret. What did I do?"

She did have a secret, one she'd planned to tell him about, but now that he would open Nan's box, she might never have to. And that thrilled her. "I'm just having a wonderful time," she said.

He grinned. "Me, too. And we haven't even seen the fireworks yet."

Isabella couldn't wait to watch the fireworks with him tonight. She loved spending time with Savannah, but she also looked forward to tonight, when she would attend the bonfire and they could have some time alone.

True, some of that time would involve him going through Nan's things, but Isabella suspected that would show him everything that she'd planned to tell him, that Nan had loved him, and Isabella was glad that her friend would get the chance, through the things she left behind, to tell him herself.

"Daddy, the parade is over. I need to get my stuff for the bonfire and spending the night!" Savannah yelled.

"If she has her things ready now," Dana

said to Titus, "she can ride back to the ranch with us."

"I have them ready," Savannah said. "Can I ride with them, Daddy? Can I, please?"

"Are you really that excited about leaving me here all alone?" he asked.

She smirked. "You're not alone, Daddy. Miss Isabella's here."

Savvy, standing a short distance behind him, winked at Isabella and mouthed, *Told you.*

Isabella managed not to laugh, but enjoyed watching Titus pick up his little girl and hug her. He said, "You know what, you're absolutely right. You can go ahead to the ranch, but make sure you listen to the rules, okay? Be very careful around that bonfire."

"I will, Daddy. Love you," she said, hugging him before he put her back on the ground.

Then, instead of heading to the house to get her bag, Savannah rushed to Isabella and wrapped her arms around her. "Love you, Miss Isabella."

She heard a soft gasp from Savvy and saw Dana's hand move to her throat as they watched the interaction. Titus, however, merely smiled and nodded.

Isabella said a prayer of thanks as she returned Savannah's hug. "Oh, Savannah, I love you too."

Titus picked up the lawn chairs from the sidewalk while Isabella gathered candy the kids had missed when grabbing the tossed treats. He liked how natural this felt, the two of them cleaning up after their friends had gone. She blended so well in his world, which reminded him that she hadn't yet officially moved to Claremont. "How long are you planning to stay at the B and B?"

She picked up a couple of Pixie Stix and tossed them in the canvas bag he'd given her for collecting the stray bits of candy. "I'd planned to stay there until I made up my mind whether this was the place I wanted to move to permanently. All of my things are still in my apartment in Atlanta, you know."

He folded another chair. "Right, I knew that much already, but that wasn't what I asked."

"What did you ask, again?" She smiled as she grabbed a Tootsie Roll from the sidewalk.

He dropped the folding chair on the stack he'd started on the porch. Then he walked toward her to help her finish gathering the last bits of candy. "I asked how long you're staying at the B and B, but what I really want to know is whether you've decided to stay in Claremont," he said, picking up a green Jolly Rancher and dropping it in her bag. "I'd assumed when you took the job at Willow's Haven that you'd find a place to live, move your things here, that type of thing."

She stopped gathering the candy and looked directly at Titus. "I guess I was waiting to make sure."

He dropped another piece of candy in the bag and stood still. He didn't want to move away from her now. "Make sure of what?" he asked, so close to her that he could see her slender throat pulse as she swallowed.

"That Claremont had everything I was looking for," she said breathily.

There was more to this conversation than her job at Willow's Haven, and he was certain they both knew it. "And? Does it?"

She nodded. "I can't imagine anywhere I'd rather be."

He couldn't imagine anywhere he'd rather her be, either. Or anywhere he'd rather be.

A car passed by, and a tap of the horn pulled them out of the moment and caused them to turn and see Jasmine Waddell slowing down, her window open and one hand waving. "Hey, Mr. Jameson!" she called. "Are y'all going to come watch the fireworks at the square? We're giving away free ice cream at the Sweet Stop!" She'd slowed her car to a complete stop while she waited for his answer.

"I think we're going to watch the fireworks from here, Jasmine, but thanks for letting us know," he said.

She nodded and grinned as though she totally approved, and then gave him a thumbs-up before driving away.

Shaking his head, he turned to Isabella. "You sure you're ready for life in a small town? There are no secrets here, you know."

A look passed over her face that he couldn't read, but then she nodded. "Yes, I'm ready. Actually, I think Claremont is exactly what I've prayed for."

There she went, mentioning prayer again, and Titus felt he should say something spiritual, but he still wasn't feeling it. However, his father's words of inspirational advice had been at the forefront of his mind throughout the day, almost as much as his words of advice about opening the box and moving beyond his past. But Titus would handle the problems in his life one at a time, and he'd start with Nan's box. "Well, I'm glad that you're here," he said, "especially today."

"When you go through Nan's things, you mean?" she asked.

He didn't want that box—and not knowing what was in it—overshadowing what could be their first true time alone together. "Yeah, that's what I mean. And I don't see any reason to keep waiting." He held his hand out, and she slid her palm against his. "Come on."

She walked beside him to the porch as though she was as apprehensive about opening the box as Titus. And maybe she was. Unable to push aside the sense of dread at what was about to happen, he led her to one of the two wicker chairs at the opposite end of the porch from the swing and began second-guessing whether it was a good decision to have Isabella here. What if, after opening the box, he didn't want to be around anyone? What if he needed time to process whatever was inside?

"Are you sure you want me here?" she

asked, apparently running through the same scenario as Titus.

But the thought of her *not* being here was more unsettling than the thought of her beside him when he ripped the bandage off that old wound. Isabella gave him comfort, made him feel as though he could truly start living again, in spite of the pain of his past. "I'm sure."

Then he went inside to retrieve the box. A moment later, he returned to the porch carrying the brown square that had plagued him the past seven days. Amazing, how something so light could press so heavy on his soul.

He set the box on the small wicker table between the chairs. Isabella reached for his hand and squeezed it gently.

"You ready?" she asked.

Titus examined the hospital address in the top left corner. Taking a deep breath, he pulled the tape away.

He opened the box, and the photograph that covered the other items hurled him back to the day the picture was taken…at their wedding.

"Oh, my," Isabella whispered. "What a beautiful picture."

"She kept our wedding picture." Titus had kept the same photo on the nightstand beside his bed for over a year after Nan left, but then the memory hurt more than it helped, and he'd put it away. He hadn't realized she'd taken a copy, and he certainly hadn't expected it to be the first thing he saw in her box.

Isabella edged closer to peer at the photo of Titus and Nan on the beach, the sun setting in the distance as they pledged their vows.

Those promises echoed clearly through his thoughts.

I promise to love and cherish you, in sickness and in health, as long as we both shall live.

He'd meant the words and kept his vow, even after she'd abandoned Titus and their little girl. Nan hadn't. Yet she'd kept this photo. "Why did she keep this?" He lifted the picture and saw the second photo, as moving as the first.

A small gasp escaped Isabella as she saw the image of mother and child, the photograph of Nan and their baby girl. "Oh, look at Savannah."

Titus remembered taking the picture in the hospital before they brought Savannah home.

Cradling her, Nan smiled at the baby in her arms as though nothing in the world could make her any happier.

"You—you can see her love for Savannah so clearly," Isabella whispered, conveying exactly what Titus felt.

Then reality set in. "But she left her," he said. What had happened between the time he took this photo and three years later, when she walked out? "It doesn't make sense." He moved that photo to the table, placed it on top of the wedding picture and then saw another item in the box. A satin pink ribbon, tied around two rings that Titus recognized immediately. Her wedding set. Along the edge of the ribbon, in Nan's handwriting, were the words, *For Savannah*.

Titus had wondered what she did with the rings after she left. Now he knew. And he still didn't understand.

The next items in the box were composed of construction paper, finger paint and Popsicle sticks, crafts from Savannah's Sunday school classes and vacation Bible schools. One had a tiny handprint in the center, a little smeared from where the teacher had obviously tried to slow the paint-covered palm of a busy two-year-old long enough to make the print on the page. Above the image were the words written by Savannah's teacher:

Happy Mother's Day, Mommy. I love you!

And then the poem at the bottom:

This is the hand you used to hold
When I was only two years old.

Titus's throat clenched. Nan had kept the photos, her wedding bands, Savannah's precious crafts and this tender Mother's Day image. And the only thing left in the box, he realized, was her Bible.

Everything had to do with their marriage, their daughter, their love.

He had no answers for why she would have walked away from the things she had obviously still cared about. No answers at all.

His throat tightened so much it hurt. His head began to throb, and his heart pounded in his chest.

He started to lift the Bible from the box but stopped when Isabella's tears fell onto his forearm. He'd been so immersed in his own emotions that he hadn't realized she'd started to cry. He looked at her now and saw that the tears continued to fall, and the fact that the items in the box affected her as much as they affected him touched him deeply.

Titus wrapped an arm around her and pulled her close, thankful that she was here with him now.

"She obviously loved you and Savannah," she whispered, "very much."

He nodded, having no choice but to agree. There was nothing in the box to point to anyone else in her life, and from all indications she *had* still loved both of them, enough that everything she left behind had to do with them and their love for each other. "I'd just hoped to learn something about why she left," he said, his voice thick and raspy as his emotions were pulled in two different directions. Part of him was thrilled to learn that Nan never stopped caring about him or their little girl. But the other part wanted to know, if she'd still cared, why had she walked away? And why hadn't she at least called when she'd known she was dying and let them say goodbye?

Isabella wiped her cheeks, cleared her

throat and then placed a hand on his forearm. "Are you okay?"

Again, he nodded, though he was more
confused than okay. But he now had to agree
with Isabella's words. Nan had loved Titus
and Savannah very much.

"Can I get you something?" she asked.
"Maybe something to drink? I could make
some tea."

He truly appreciated her wanting to help
him deal with the blow of still not knowing
what happened. "Some tea would be great."

She lifted the photo of Nan holding Savannah in the hospital before placing it back on
the table and heading inside for the tea.

Titus also looked at that photo and at the
wedding picture, and at every other item.
Then he reached for the last thing in the box,
Nan's weathered Bible. And as he lifted it,
he noticed several papers sticking out from
within the pages. He placed the Bible in his
lap and opened it to the first thick paper,
which he now saw was an envelope, with a
single name in Nan's swirling handwriting in
the center—*Titus*.

And once again his heart thudded solidly in
his chest. Taking a deep breath, he withdrew

the single sheet of paper from the envelope
and began to read.

Dear Titus,

Hurting you was the last thing I ever intended to do. Sometimes, God gives us
tough decisions to make, and maybe I
made the wrong one. I thought I could
handle anything, that we could handle
anything, but I learned my limitations.
Leaving you and our precious Savannah wasn't something I'd have ever anticipated, but I also didn't want you to
watch what I knew would happen over
the next months. Months that, as it turns
out, have turned into years.

As I'm writing this letter, I know that
my time here is nearly over. I can feel
God calling me home. It has been almost three years since I left our home
and walked away from the two people I
love more than any others, you and Savannah. I never ever stopped loving you.
I want you to know that. I didn't think
I'd be here this long away from you. But
God kept me here longer than the doctors had thought possible, and for that I

am grateful, because it gave Him time to answer my most vital prayer.

I've met someone…

Titus read the next lines with undeniable shock. "No," he said, shaking his head in disbelief. "No."

The screen door creaked as Isabella exited carrying two glasses of iced tea. She started toward Titus, still holding the letter in his hand and looking at the second woman who'd totally crushed his heart.

"You…" He forced the word from his throat, his head hammering so fiercely he wasn't sure he could finish, but he couldn't stop now, "You—knew Nan."

The glasses shattered as they collided with the porch, tea and ice splashing at her feet amid the broken glass.

"Titus," she said, her eyes wide with panic as she stared at the letter in his hand, "I'm—so sorry. I wanted to tell you. I almost did, but I thought—I thought if you just opened the box, then you'd know everything that…"

He shook his head. "Stop. If you'd wanted to tell me, you would have. No more lies,

Isabella. I've had enough for a lifetime, and I don't need any more from you."

"Titus," she breathed, "please, let me explain. Please."

She wanted to explain? Explain what? Listening to him talk about his wife, about his confusion over her leaving and about how painful it had been having her leave without any explanation.

When Isabella knew exactly why she had left?

"You can't explain. There's no explanation for you keeping that from me, none at all."

"Titus, I care about you, and I care about Savannah," she said, her tears flowing fiercely now.

It infuriated him that, even now, knowing she'd lied the entire time she'd been in Claremont, he still didn't want to see her cry. "We don't have anything else to talk about, Isabella."

Then, for the second time in his life, a woman that he loved walked away.

The difference was…this time he had to watch her go.

Chapter Fourteen

But true love can also bring pain.

As he'd done several times throughout yesterday afternoon, last night and this morning, Titus reread Nan's letter, specifically the part that had completely thrown his world off-kilter.

I've met someone…she's become the sister I never had, a true friend that has been with me through the worst of this disease. Her name is Isabella Gray, and I honestly think God sent her to me as an answered prayer. Three years ago, I was given six months to live. And the doctors believed those six months would be a rapid deterioration of my quality of life, something that would undoubtedly be difficult on me and my family.

I didn't want that for you. I didn't want your memories of me to include watching me die. I wanted you to remember the happy times, the love that we shared. When I learned what was happening, I didn't know how to tell you the truth, and I didn't want to lie. So I left.

And I prayed.

I prayed for God to watch over you and Savannah, and I prayed for Him to somehow let me know that you would both be loved, the way I had planned to love you, always. I wanted to be a good wife. I wanted to be a good mom. But if I couldn't be with you, then I wanted someone there who would love you the way that I would.

Isabella is a beautiful person, inside and out. By now, you've met her and have seen the sweet spirit that I've known for the last six months. She has so much pain in her past, and she deserves love. Titus, she deserves you. Isabella has never had real love. She's never had the love of a man who loves completely, like

you do. And she's never known the love
of a child. I know she will fall in love
with Savannah. And in all honesty, she'll
be a wonderful mother. No, I don't want
Savannah to forget me—I have left my
wedding rings for her, as well as a letter
that I want you to give her on her wedding day. But I want her to have a mother
figure after I'm gone, and I do believe
God sent Isabella to me to fulfill my request, to let me know that you and Savannah would be loved.

If I'd have known then—when I left—
what I know now, I would have stayed
longer. I have lived well past the time
they'd given, but then I would have
risked you seeing me die. And I didn't
want that.

I've included a letter for Isabella, too.
Please give it to my dear, sweet friend.
My heart has never been so torn. I pray
Savannah will forgive me. I pray you
will forgive me, too. And I pray that Isabella will forgive me. I lied to her. I
am not proud of this truth, but I knew
if I'd told her we were still married,
she'd have called you during these final

months. She'd have wanted you to get the chance to say goodbye. And I didn't tell her about Savannah for the same reason. Isabella didn't know her own parents. She was orphaned, and her story tore at my heart. So I knew she'd want Savannah to say goodbye, too. I pray she'll understand that I didn't want you to see me this way, frail and sick and at death's door.

Please, Titus, remember how much I loved you, because I never stopped. Remind our little girl that I loved her dearly, and I always will. And, if God did send Isabella to me because she's meant for you, love her. Don't hold back because of me. I want you to be loved. It's what I always wanted, honestly.

True love brings happiness, more joy than I'd have thought possible. But true love can also bring pain. Leaving you was more painful than any disease. But loving you and loving Savannah has seen me through.

I do love you,

Nan

Titus placed the envelope for Savannah's wedding day in the box with the other items. He picked up the third envelope that Nan had left in her Bible and stared at the name on the outside.

Isabella.

If he were a revengeful man, he'd keep the letter. She'd withheld the truth about Nan from him since the day they met. He could withhold this truth from her...if he were an unforgiving man.

And if, throughout the night, he hadn't continued to remember her crying and leaving.

He wasn't ready to see her, wasn't ready to forgive her, not yet. But Nan had admittedly lied to her, and Isabella, like Titus, deserved the truth. He grabbed his truck keys and the final letter and headed out the door.

Isabella placed another blouse in her suitcase. She was no longer crying because she had no tears left. And she'd almost finished packing, preparing to leave the town and the people she cared so much about. And the man she'd come to love.

You knew Nan.

She couldn't get Titus's words, or the pain

they'd held, out of her mind or her heart. Why hadn't she told him the truth? And what had Nan said in that letter?

Obviously, Isabella couldn't stay here. To be near Titus and Savannah would only remind her of what she'd never have. A real family. She'd had a tiny glimpse and had even, over the past day, had a glimmer of hope that it might be part of God's plan, that she would finally have the kind of family she'd dreamed of, with Titus and Savannah.

But that wasn't His plan, and she'd been foolish to think that she could've gone forward with any kind of relationship with Titus when she'd lied to him from the day she met him. She hoped Savvy understood why she could no longer work at Willow's Haven.

A knock at her door caused her to drop the next blouse. She crossed her room and found Annette Tingle, the sweet lady who ran the B and B with her husband, on the other side.

"You didn't want breakfast this morning?" she asked.

Isabella shook her head. Her stomach had been so upset since she left Titus yesterday afternoon that she couldn't even think of eating. "No, ma'am," she said.

Annette frowned at the suitcase on the bed. "You aren't leaving, are you?"

"I was going to tell you later," Isabella said, struggling to make her voice sound as normal as possible, as though she had some idea of where to go and what to do when she left Claremont. In truth, she suspected she'd head back to her apartment in Atlanta and mourn the loss of yet another important person in her life. This time, it wasn't her best friend, but the man that she truly believed she'd started to love. And the little girl who had completely claimed her heart.

"Oh, my, we sure will miss you around here," Annette said. She held up an envelope. "Maybe that's why Titus dropped this off for you?"

Isabella focused on the envelope, and her name written on the outside. That was not a man's handwriting, and she suspected she knew exactly who'd written it. "Thank you," she managed, her hand trembling as she accepted the envelope from Annette and then closed the door.

Moving to sit on the edge of the bed, she opened the envelope and read the words from her friend.

Dear Isabella,

By now, I am sure you have met Titus and our precious Savannah. I have no doubt you were confused and surprised to learn that Titus and I weren't divorced, as I led you to believe. Please forgive me. I deceived you, and I hate that I did that to someone who I adore so much. You are the sister I never had, the best friend I always wanted, and I love you, truly.

Knowing your past, the pain of your childhood without parents and the struggles of your marriage to Richard, I knew you wouldn't understand why I didn't want to see Titus now, why I didn't want to see Savannah. I knew you'd want them to be able to say goodbye, but please try to understand. I couldn't bear the thought of them seeing me like this. I want them to remember me the way I was, the way we were, when I was healthy and happy and whole.

The doctors couldn't understand why I continued to live, when every test and every statistic said I shouldn't be here now. But I know why I'm still here. I prayed to God to show me that Titus and

Savannah would be loved, and He sent
you. I know that with all of my heart,
and I want you to know that, should you
and Titus find the love that I believe you
can share, I am happy for you, happy for
him and most definitely happy for my
dear, sweet Savannah.

Love them, Isabella. And know, always, that you were a true friend and
that you were also loved by me.

Nan

Isabella thought she had no tears left, but
she'd thought wrong. They pushed free now,
with the knowledge of how very much she
was loved by her friend and how terribly she'd
messed up in not telling Titus the truth. Nan
had known she'd fall in love with Titus. She'd
known that she'd love Savannah. And she'd
sent Isabella to Claremont with the purpose
of setting that love in motion while believing
that God had answered her prayer.

But Isabella hadn't been able to tell him the
truth, and because of that, she'd hurt him. She
couldn't stop seeing his face with that pained,
tormented expression as he held Nan's letter.

Nan's departure had stabbed his heart deeply, but Isabella's betrayal twisted the knife.

How could she have so terribly hurt the man she cared about more than any other?

She folded the letter, placed it back in the envelope and turned it to look at her name in Nan's handwriting. In spite of being hurt by Isabella, Titus had brought her this letter. Obviously, he hadn't forgiven her, because he'd merely left the letter with Mrs. Tingle. But he'd still brought it, which meant that maybe, deep down, he still cared.

Isabella looked at the suitcase on the bed. She didn't want to leave Claremont, didn't want to leave Willow's Haven, or Savvy and her other new friends, or the church that felt like home. She didn't want to leave the sweet little girl who reminded her so much of herself. And she didn't want to leave Titus.

Love them, Isabella.

"Oh, Nan," she whispered, "I already do."

She closed her eyes and prayed, *God, give me the courage to do what I need to do. And Lord, if it be Your will, let him find it in his heart to forgive me.*

Then she started toward the door.

* * *

Titus hadn't known his destination after he left Nan's letter for Isabella at the B and B, or at least he hadn't thought he had a destination in mind. Yet his truck never veered from the path that brought him here, and in his heart, he'd known where he was going all along.

Sitting on a pew in the center of the church that had always been such a fundamental part of his life, Titus couldn't fathom how, when he hit rock bottom, he hadn't come here first, hadn't turned to God when he needed Him most.

Nan said in her letter that she prayed for him to love Isabella. And Titus knew God had answered that prayer, because he did love her, truly. He'd done his best to fight it, to deny what he felt or downplay it as mere attraction, but he had no doubt that he had fallen in love with the woman who he now knew had befriended Nan. But the pain of her dishonesty was so fierce that he didn't know if he could get past it.

He looked to the pulpit and could almost hear the phrase Brother Henry had used from time to time when talking about true forgiveness. "Too many people say they bury the hatchet and leave the handle sticking out."

"God, help me here. I've been so mad at You, and I'm sorry. I've needed You more than ever, and I've been too stubborn to ask for help. I thought I could handle everything on my own, but I can't, especially not now, with what's happened with Isabella. Help me to move past the pain, Lord. And help me, dear God, to forgive. I—" he sucked in a breath at the power of the words "—I don't want to lose her, too."

He sensed more than heard the door to the auditorium slowly open, and when he turned he expected to find Brother Henry or one of the elderly women who cleaned the building. But, in spite of his recent defiance, God had obviously answered his prayer without hesitation.

Isabella timidly stepped into the auditorium, as though afraid he would tell her to leave.

That wasn't happening. Never again. His heart, his soul, had ached ever since he watched her go yesterday, and he never wanted to see her leave again.

"I'm so sorry," she said. "I should have

told you the truth, and I didn't." She slowly walked down the aisle toward him, still acting as though she expected him to send her away. "And I started packing my things. I was going to leave and do my best not to hurt you by staying." She moved closer, her head shaking as she added, "But I couldn't. I don't want to leave Claremont, don't want to leave Willow's Haven or Savannah or—" Her breath caught in a gasp as she reached his pew. "And I don't want to leave you, Titus. I—I love you."

Awed at how much he'd already missed her in his life, Titus stood, cupped her face in his hands and thought about everything he knew about this woman that God had undoubtedly placed in his life…through Nan. And about everything he still wanted to know. They were just starting their journey together, and he didn't want it to end.

"I don't want you to leave," he said. "I knew that yesterday, but I was too angry and too hurt to stop you. But I can't lose you, Isabella. I love you, too."

Amazed at the instant flood of happiness in his heart, Titus knew he was exactly where he was supposed to be, in this church with

Isabella in his life. And, after weeks of thinking about her and knowing how very much he
cared, he wrapped his arms around her and
tenderly kissed the woman he loved.

Isabella had often wondered what it'd be
like to be in Titus's arms. She'd dreamed
about this kiss. And she'd prayed for his love.

It was better than she'd ever expected. And
her excitement, happiness, pure unharnessed
joy caused her to release a surge of delighted
giggles as soon as the kiss ended.

Titus, obviously surprised by her reaction,
asked, "I take it that means you liked it?"

She laughed. "I'm not sure. You may need
to do it again."

He did, and she could feel the smile on
his lips through the kiss, because it totally
matched her own. Oh, how God had blessed
her with Nan's friendship, and with Titus's
love.

Thank You, thank You, thank You.

Titus touched her chin. "You didn't tell me
how you knew I was here."

She felt foolish now for what she'd done,
but she'd tell him the truth, about this and
about everything else from now on. "I went

to your house, and when your truck wasn't there, I drove around town until I found it."

His laughter echoed through the auditorium. "Sure didn't take you long to get used to small-town life, did it?"

She smiled, because God had answered that prayer, too. "I think I could stay here forever."

"Can't imagine anything I'd want more."

Epilogue

"Miss Isabella, can we do these ribbons in my hair for school sometime, too? Like for picture day?"

Savannah tilted her head to the side as she examined her reflection in the standing oval mirror in the church's dressing room. She looked so pretty in the tea-length dress, the same deep maroon as the gerbera daisies in her bouquet. The ribbons in her hair were maroon and deep gold, complementing the colors that decorated the church and reception hall for the October wedding. Titus hadn't wanted a long engagement, and neither had Isabella. She couldn't wait to be his wife.

"We can definitely do ribbons for picture day," Isabella said, as Savannah spun around in the dress while taking in her reflection again in the mirror. She was so happy today, which warmed Isabella's heart. It was hard to believe that this was the same little girl who'd been so sad when Isabella met her merely four months ago.

A tap sounded at the door, and Titus's father peeked in. He grinned at Savannah, still spinning in front of the mirror. "You know, if you keep that up, you may be too dizzy to walk down the aisle, and it's almost time for you to get started."

Savannah stopped and actually did take a little sidestep before giggling and touching her head. "Okay, I'm stopping, Pops."

He winked. "Probably a good idea." Then he said, "Hey, I think that's the beginning of your music."

"Oh, it is!" Savannah turned to Isabella. "This is so much fun, isn't it?"

Isabella couldn't agree more. "So much fun," she said.

Savannah started to leave but stopped near the door. "Miss Isabella?"

"Yes?"

"Does this mean…" She looked at her grandfather and then back to Isabella, "Can I call you Mommy now?"

How Isabella loved this little girl. And how her tender question touched her heart. "Oh, Savannah, I would like that very much."

She rushed back across the room and hugged Isabella. "I love you," she whispered, "Mommy."

Then, while Isabella tried to get a grip on her heart, Savannah left, and Titus's dad, wiping away tears of his own, asked, "You know your cue?" He and Titus's mother had been wonderful to help her plan the wedding and to be here over the past week as they got everything ready for the big day. Truthfully, she had adored both of them from the moment she met them. They had treated her with love, and she was already beginning to feel a part of their precious family.

She nodded. "I believe I do." They'd practiced last night at the rehearsal, with Brother Henry and his wife, Mary, making sure they knew exactly what to do. It was a small wedding, with just their friends from Claremont present. But their friends, it turned out, ended up including the majority of the town.

"Well, in case you forget, I wanted to offer to go along."

Isabella blinked. "Go along?"

He lifted a shoulder. "Didn't really seem right, you walking down the aisle by yourself and all. I wanted to ask if you'd mind having an escort? I'd sure love to have the honor."

She couldn't speak, but she nodded.

Smiling, he tilted his head toward the auditorium. "I think that's our cue." Then he took her hand, slid it into place at the crook of his arm and walked her to the auditorium doors. "Isabella Jameson," he said, nodding. "I like the sound of that."

The doors opened, and she saw Titus, the man she loved, the answer to her prayers, waiting at the front of the church. "I like the sound of it, too."

* * * * *

Dear Reader,

I wrote my first book about orphaned children (*Daddy Wanted*, February 2014) to bring attention to the love and care children need when they've lost their earthly parents. The story had a special spot in my heart because my grandsons lost their birth parents when they were merely four and five years old. Watching my son and daughter-in-law become parents to our precious grandboys touched me so deeply that I wanted to share the joy of helping children like Alanus and Jerry with you.

The Willow's Haven series shares stories about orphaned or abandoned children who survive even the most difficult circumstances with love from God and His children. I cried several times writing this book, and I know I'll probably cry through each book of the series. The message and stories are that close to my heart. I pray that more children who've lost parents find God's love through the love of His children.

Follow the Willow's Haven series, as well as my other novels, via my website, reneeandrews.com, Facebook page, facebook.com/

AuthorReneeAndrews, and Twitter, @Renee-
Andrews. And you'll see pictures of Alanus
and Jerry there, too. See if their smiles don't
put one on your face. I know they keep a
smile on mine!

If you have prayer requests, let me know.
I'll lift your request up to the Lord in prayer.
I love to hear from readers, so please write
to me at renee@reneeandrews.com or at PO
Box 8, Gadsden, AL 35902. I also enjoy visiting book clubs reading my novels, either
personally or via Skype. Send your book club
request; I'll provide discussion questions and
do my best to be a part of your club's meeting.

Blessings in Christ,
Renee Andrews

LARGER-PRINT BOOKS!

GET 2 FREE LARGER-PRINT NOVELS PLUS 2 FREE MYSTERY GIFTS

Love Inspired®
SUSPENSE
RIVETING INSPIRATIONAL ROMANCE

Larger-print novels are now available...

LISLP15

REQUEST YOUR FREE BOOKS!
2 FREE WHOLESOME ROMANCE NOVELS IN LARGER PRINT
PLUS 2 FREE MYSTERY GIFTS

☆☆☆☆☆☆☆☆☆☆☆☆☆☆☆☆☆☆☆☆☆☆☆☆

HEARTWARMING™

☆☆☆☆☆☆☆☆☆☆☆☆☆☆☆☆☆☆☆☆☆☆☆☆

Wholesome, tender romances

YES! Please send me 2 FREE Harlequin® Heartwarming Larger-Print novels and my 2 FREE mystery gifts (gifts worth about $10). After receiving them, if I don't wish to receive any more books, I can return the shipping statement marked "cancel." If I don't cancel, I will receive 4 brand-new larger-print novels every month and be billed just $5.24 per book in the U.S. or $5.99 per book in Canada. That's a savings of at least 19% off the cover price. It's quite a bargain! Shipping and handling is just 50¢ per book in the U.S. and 75¢ per book in Canada.* I understand that accepting the 2 free books and gifts places me under no obligation to buy anything. I can always return a shipment and cancel at any time. Even if I never buy another book, the two free books and gifts are mine to keep forever.

161/361 IDN GHX2

Name	(PLEASE PRINT)

Address		Apt. #

City	State/Prov..	Zip/Postal Code

Signature (if under 18, a parent or guardian must sign)

Mail to the **Reader Service**:
IN U.S.A.: P.O. Box 1867, Buffalo, NY 14240-1867
IN CANADA: P.O. Box 609, Fort Erie, Ontario L2A 5X3

* Terms and prices subject to change without notice. Prices do not include applicable taxes. Sales tax applicable in N.Y. Canadian residents will be charged applicable taxes. Offer not valid in Quebec. This offer is limited to one order per household. Not valid for current subscribers to Harlequin Heartwarming larger-print books. All orders subject to credit approval. Credit or debit balances in a customer's account(s) may be offset by any other outstanding balance owed by or to the customer. Please allow 4 to 6 weeks for delivery. Offer available while quantities last.

Your Privacy—The Reader Service is committed to protecting your privacy. Our Privacy Policy is available online at www.ReaderService.com or upon request from the Reader Service.

We make a portion of our mailing list available to reputable third parties that offer products we believe may interest you. If you prefer that we not exchange your name with third parties, or if you wish to clarify or modify your communication preferences, please visit us at www.ReaderService.com/consumerchoice or write to us at Reader Service Preference Service, P.O. Box 9062, Buffalo, NY 14240-9062. Include your complete name and address.

READERSERVICE.COM

Manage your account online!

- Review your order history
- Manage your payments
- Update your address

We've designed the Reader Service website just for you.

Enjoy all the features!

- Discover new series available to you, and read excerpts from any series.
- Respond to mailings and special monthly offers.
- Connect with favorite authors at the blog.
- Browse the Bonus Bucks catalog and online-only exculsives.
- Share your feedback.

Visit us at:

ReaderService.com

RS15

YES! Please send me **The Montana Mavericks Collection** in Larger Print. This collection begins with 3 FREE books and 2 FREE gifts (gifts valued at approx. $20.00 retail) in the first shipment, along with the other first 4 books from the collection! If I do not cancel, I will receive 8 monthly shipments until I have the entire 51-book Montana Mavericks collection. I will receive 2 or 3 FREE books in each shipment and I will pay just $4.99 US/ $5.89 CDN for each of the other four books in each shipment, plus $2.99 for shipping and handling per shipment.*If I decide to keep the entire collection, I'll have paid for only 32 books, because 19 books are FREE! I understand that accepting the 3 free books and gifts places me under no obligation to buy anything. I can always return a shipment and cancel at any time. My free books and gifts are mine to keep no matter what I decide.

263 HCN 2404   463 HCN 2404

Name	(PLEASE PRINT)	
Address		Apt. #
City	State/Prov.	Zip/Postal Code

Signature (if under 18, a parent or guardian must sign)

Mail to the **Reader Service:**
IN U.S.A.: P.O. Box 1867, Buffalo, NY 14240-1867
IN CANADA: P.O. Box 609, Fort Erie, Ontario L2A 5X3

* Terms and prices subject to change without notice. Prices do not include applicable taxes. Sales tax applicable in N.Y. Canadian residents will be charged applicable taxes. This offer is limited to one order per household. All orders subject to approval. Credit or debit balances in a customer's account(s) may be offset by any other outstanding balance owed by or to the customer. Please allow 4 to 6 weeks for delivery. Offer available while quantities last. Offer not available to Quebec residents.